I0749284

The Inside Of The Cup

Volume 6

Winston Churchill

The Inside Of The Cup, Vol 6.

Winston Churchill

PO Box 2211
Fairfield, IA 52556
www.1stworldlibrary.org
First Edition

LCCN: 2003099818

Softcover ISBN: 1-59540-144-X
Hardcover ISBN: 1-4218-0694-0
eBook ISBN: 1-59540-194-6

The Inside Of The Cup, Vol 6.

contributed by Ed ,Tim & Rodney

in support of

1st World Library Literary Society

TABLE OF CONTENTS

Volume 6

CHAPTER XX

THE ARRAIGNMENT

I

Looking backward, Hodder perceived that he had really come to the momentous decision of remaining at St. John's in the twilight of an evening when, on returning home from seeing Kate Marcy at Mr. Bentley's he had entered the darkening church. It was then that his mission had appeared to him as a vision. Every day, afterward, his sense and knowledge of this mission had grown stronger.

To his mind, not the least of the trials it was to impose upon him, and one which would have to be dealt with shortly, was a necessary talk with his assistant, McCrae. If their relationship had from the beginning been unusual and unsatisfactory, adjectives would seem to defy what it had become during the summer. What did McCrae think of him? For Hodder had, it will be recalled, bidden his assistant good-by - and then had remained. At another brief interview, during which McCrae had betrayed no surprise, uttered no censure or comment, Hodder had announced his determination to remain in the city, and to take no part in the services. An announcement sufficiently astounding. During the months that followed, they had met, at rare intervals, exchanged casual greetings, and passed on. And yet Hodder had the feeling, more firmly planted than ever, that McCrae was awaiting, with an interest which might be called suspense, the culmination of the process going on within him.

Well, now that he had worked it out, now that he had reached his decision, it was incumbent upon him to tell his assistant what that decision was. Hodder shrank from it as from an ordeal. His affection for the man, his admiration for McCrae's faithful, untiring, and unrecognized services had deepened. He had a theory that McCrae really liked him - would even sympathize with his solution; yet he procrastinated. He was afraid to put his theory to the test. It was not that Hodder feared that his own solution was not the right one, but that McCrae might not find it so: he was intensely concerned that it should also be McCrae's solution - the answer, if one liked, to McCrae's mute and eternal questionings. He wished to have it a fruition for McCrae as well as for himself; since theoretically, at least, he had pierced the hard crust of his assistant's exterior, and conceived him beneath to be all suppressed fire. In short, Hodder wished to go into battle side by side with McCrae. Therein lay his anxiety.

Another consideration troubled him - McCrae's family, dependent on a rather meagre salary. His assistant, in sustaining him in the struggle he meant to enter, would be making even a greater sacrifice than himself. For Hodder had no illusions, and knew that the odds against him were incalculable. Whatever, if defeated, his own future might be, McCrae's was still more problematical and tragic.

The situation, when it came, was even more difficult than Hodder had imagined it, since McCrae was not a man to oil the wheels of conversation. In silence he followed the rector up the stairs and into his study, in silence he took the seat at the opposite side of the table. And Hodder, as he hesitated over his opening, contemplated in no little perplexity and travail the gaunt and non-committal face before him:

"McCrae," he began at length, "you must have thought my conduct this summer most peculiar. I wish to thank you, first of all, for the consideration you have shown me, and to tell you how deeply I appreciate your taking the entire burden of the work of the parish."

McCrae shook his head vigorously, but did not speak.

"I owe it to you to give you some clew to what happened to me," the rector continued, "although I have an idea that you do not need much enlightenment on this matter. I have a feeling that you have somehow been aware of my discouragement during the past year or so, and of the causes of it. You yourself hold ideals concerning the Church which you have not confided to me. Of this I am sure. I came here to St. John's full of hope and confidence, gradually to lose both, gradually to realise that there was something wrong with me, that in spite of all my efforts I was unable to make any headway in the right direction. I became perplexed, dissatisfied - the results were so meagre, so out of proportion to the labour. And the very fact that those who may be called our chief parishioners had no complaint merely added to my uneasiness. That kind of success didn't satisfy me, and I venture to assume it didn't satisfy you."

Still McCrae made no sign.

"Finally I came to what may be termed a double conclusion. In the first place, I began to see more and more clearly that our modern civilization is at fault, to perceive how completely it is conducted on the materialistic theory of the survival of the fittest rather than that of the brotherhood of man, and that those who mainly support this church are, consciously or not, using it as a bulwark for the privilege they have gained at the expense of their fellow-citizens. And my conclusion was that Christianity must contain some vital germ which I had somehow missed, and which I must find if I could, and preach and release it. That it was the release of this germ these people feared unconsciously. I say to you, at the risk of the accusation of conceit, that I believed myself to have a power in the pulpit if I could only discover the truth."

Hodder thought he detected, as he spoke these words, a certain relaxation of the tension.

"For a while, as the result of discouragement, of cowardice, I may say, of the tearing-down process of the theological structure - built of debris from many ruins on which my conception of Christianity rested, I lost all faith. For many weeks I did not enter the church, as you yourself must know. Then, when I had given up all hope, through certain incidents and certain persona, a process of reconstruction began. In short, through no virtue which I can claim as my own, I believe I have arrived at the threshold of an understanding of Christianity as our Lord taught it and lived it. And I intend to take the pulpit and begin to preach it.

"I am deeply concerned in regard to yourself as to what effect my course may have on you. And I am not you to listen to me with a view that you should see your way clear to support me McCrae, but rather that you should be fully apprised of my new belief and intentions. I owe this to you, for your loyal support in the pest. I shall go over with you, later, if you care to listen, my whole position. It may be called the extreme Protestant position, and I use protestant, for want of a better word, to express what I believe is Paul's true as distinguished from the false of his two inconsistent theologies. It was this doctrine of Paul's of redemption by faith, of reacting grace by an inevitable spiritual law - of rebirth, if you will - that Luther and the Protestant reformers revived and recognized, rightly, as the vital element of Christ's teachings, although they did not succeed in separating it wholly from the dross which clung to it. It is the leaven which has changed governments, and which in the end, I am firmly convinced, will make true democracy inevitable. And those who oppose democracy inherently dread its workings.

"I do not know your views, but it is only fair to add at this time that I no longer believe in the external and imposed authority of the Church in the sense in which I formerly accepted it, nor in the virgin birth, nor in certain other dogmas in which I once acquiesced. Other clergymen of our communion have proclaimed, in speech and writing, their disbelief in these things. I have satisfied my conscience as they have, and I mean to make no secret of my change. I am convinced that not one man or woman in ten thousand to-day who has rejected Christianity ever knew what Christianity is. The science and archaic philosophy in which Christianity has been swaddled and hampered is discredited, and the conclusion is drawn that Christianity itself must be discredited."

"Ye're going to preach all this?" McCrae demanded, almost fiercely.

"Yes," Hodder replied, still uncertain as to his assistant's attitude, "and more. I have fully reflected, and I am willing to accept all the consequences. I understand perfectly, McCrae, that the promulgation alone of the liberal orthodoxy of which I have spoken will bring me into conflict with the majority of the vestry and the congregation, and that the bishop will be appealed to. They will say, in effect, that I have cheated them, that they hired one man and that another has turned up, whom they never would have hired. But that won't be the whole story. If it were merely a question of doctrine, I should resign. It's deeper than that, more sinister." Hodder doubled up his hand, and laid it on the table. "It's a matter," he said, looking into McCrae's eyes, "of freeing this church from those who now hold it in chains. And the two questions, I see clearly now, the doctrinal and the economic, are so interwoven as to be inseparable. My former, ancient presentation of Christianity left men and women cold. It did not draw them into this church and send them out again fired with the determination to bring religion into everyday life, resolved to do their part in the removal of the injustices and cruelties with which we are surrounded, to bring Christianity into government, where it belongs. Don't misunderstand me I'm not going to preach politics, but religion."

"I don't misunderstand ye," answered McCrae. He leaned a little forward, staring at the rector from behind his steel spectacles with a glance which had become piercing.

"And I am going to discourage a charity which is a mockery of Christianity," Hodder went on, "the spectacle of which turns thousands of men and women in sickening revolt against the Church of Christ to-day. I have discovered, at last, how some of these persons have made their money, and are making it. And I am going to let them know, since they have repudiated God in their own souls, since they have denied the Christian principle of individual responsibility, that I, as the vicar of God, will not be a party to the transaction of using the Church as a means of doling out ill-gotten gains to the poor."

"Mr. Parr!" McCrae exclaimed.

"Yes," said the rector, slowly, and with a touch of sadness, "since you have mentioned him, Mr. Parr. But I need not say that this must go no farther. I am in possession of definite facts in regard to Mr. Parr which I shall present to him when he returns."

"Ye'll tell him to his face?"

"It is the only way."

McCrae had risen. A remarkable transformation had come over the man, - he was reminiscent, at that moment, of some Covenanter ancestor going into battle. And his voice shook with excitement.

"Ye may count on me, Mr. Hodder," he cried. "These many years I've waited, these many years I've seen what ye see now, but I was not the man. Aye, I've watched ye, since the day ye first set foot in this church. I knew what was going on inside of ye, because it was just that I felt myself. I hoped - I prayed ye might come to it."

The sight of this taciturn Scotchman, moved in this way, had an extraordinary effect on Hodder himself, and his own emotion was so inexpressibly stirred that he kept silence a moment to control it. This proof of the truth of his theory in regard to McCrae he found overwhelming.

"But you said nothing, McCrae," he began presently. "I felt all along that you knew what was wrong - if you had only spoken."

"I could not," said McCrae. "I give ye my word I tried, but I just could not. Many's the time I wanted to - but I said to myself, when I looked at you, 'wait, it will come, much better than ye can say it.' And ye have made me see more than I saw, Mr. Hodder, - already ye have. Ye've got the whole thing in ye're eye, and I only had a part of it. It's because ye're the bigger man of the two."

"You thought I'd come to it?" demanded Hodder, as though the full force of this insight had just struck him.

"Well," said McCrae, "I hoped. It seemed, to look at ye, ye'r true nature - what was by rights inside of ye. That's the best explaining I can do. And I call to mind that time ye spoke about not making the men in the classes Christians - that was what started me to thinking."

"And you asked me," returned the rector, "how welcome some of them would be in Mr. Parr's Pew."

"Ah, it worried me," declared the assistant, with characteristic frankness, "to see how deep ye were getting in with him."

Hodder did not reply to this. He had himself risen, and stood looking at McCrae, filled with a new thought.

"There is one thing I should like to say to you - which is very difficult, McCrae, but I have no doubt you see the matter as clearly as I do. In making this fight, I have no one but myself to consider. I am a single man - "

"Yell not need to go on," answered McCrae, with an odd mixture of sternness and gentleness in his voice. "I'll stand and fall with ye, Mr. Hodder. Before I ever thought of the Church I learned a trade, as a boy in Scotland. I'm not a bad carpenter. And if worse comes to worse, I've an idea I can make as much with my hands as I make in the ministry."

The smile they exchanged across the table sealed the compact between them.

II

The electric car which carried him to his appointment with the financier shot westward like a meteor through the night. And now that the hour was actually at hand, it seemed to Hodder that he was absurdly unprepared to meet it. New and formidable aspects, hitherto unthought of, rose in his mind, and the figure of Eldon Parr loomed to Brobdingnagian proportions as he approached it. In spite of his determination, the life-blood of his confidence ebbed, a sense of the power and might of the man who had now become his adversary increased; and that apprehension of the impact of the great banker's personality, the cutting edge with the vast achievements wedged in behind it, each adding weight and impetus to its momentum the apprehension he had felt in less degree on the day of the first meeting, and which had almost immediately evaporated - surged up in him now. His fear was lest the charged atmosphere of the banker's presence might deflect his own hitherto clear perception of true worth. He dreaded, once in the midst of those disturbing currents, a bungling presentation of the cause which inspired him, and which he knew to be righteousness itself.

Suddenly his mood shifted, betraying still another weakness, and he saw Eldon Parr, suddenly, vividly - more vividly, indeed, than ever before - in the shades of the hell of his loneliness. And pity welled up, drowning the image of incarnate greed and selfishness and lust for wealth and power: The unique pathos of his former relationship with the man reasserted itself, and Hodder was conscious once more of the dependence which Eldon Parr had had on his friendship. During that friendship he, Hodder, had never lost the sense of being the stronger of the two, of being leaned upon: leaned upon by a man whom the world feared and hated, and whom he had been enable to regard with anything but compassion and the unquestionable affection which sprang from it. Appalled by this transition, he alighted from the car, and stood for a moment alone in the darkness gazing at the great white houses that rose above the dusky outline of shrubbery and trees.

At any rate, he wouldn't find that sense of dependence to-night. And it steeled him somewhat to think, as he resumed his steps, that he would meet now the other side, the hard side hitherto always turned away. Had he needed no other warning of this, the answer to his note asking for an appointment would have been enough, - a brief and formal communication signed by the banker's secretary. . .

"Mr. Parr is engaged just at present, sir," said the servant who opened the door. "Would you be good enough to step into the library?"

Hardly had he entered the room when he heard a sound behind him, and turned to confront Alison. The thought of her, too, had complicated infinitely his emotions concerning the interview before him, and the sight of her now, of her mature beauty displayed in evening dress, of her white throat gleaming whiter against the severe black of her gown, made him literally speechless. Never had he accused her of boldness, and now least of all. It was the quality of her splendid courage that was borne in upon him once more above the host of other feelings and impressions, for he read in her eyes a knowledge of the meaning of his visit.

They stood facing each other an appreciable moment.

"Mr. Langmaid is with him now," she said, in a low voice.

"Yes," he answered.

Her eyes still rested on his face, questioningly, appraisingly, as though she were seeking to estimate his preparedness for the ordeal before him, his ability to go through with it successfully, triumphantly. And in her mention of Langmaid he recognized that she had meant to sound a note of warning. She had intimated a consultation of the captains, a council of war. And yet he had never spoken to her of this visit. This proof of her partisanship, that she had come to him at the crucial instant, overwhelmed him.

"You know why I am here?" he managed to say. It had to do with the extent of her knowledge.

"Oh, why shouldn't I?" she cried, "after what you have told me. And could you think I didn't understand, from the beginning, that it meant this?"

His agitation still hampered him. He made a gesture of assent.

"It was inevitable," he said.

"Yes, it' was inevitable," she assented, and walked slowly to the mantel, resting her hand on it and bending her head. "I felt that you would not shirk it, and yet I realize how painful it must be to you."

"And to you," he replied quickly.

"Yes, and to me. I do not know what you know, specifically, - I have never sought to find out things, in detail. That would be horrid. But I understand - in general - I have understood for many years." She raised her head, and flashed him a glance that was between a quivering smile and tears. "And I know that you have certain specific information."

He could only wonder at her intuition.

"So far as I am concerned, it is not for the world," he answered.

"Oh, I appreciate that in you!" she exclaimed. "I wished you to know it. I wished you to know," she added, a little unsteadily, "how much I admire you for what you are doing. They are afraid of you - they will crush you if they can."

He did not reply.

"But you are going to speak the truth," she continued, her voice low and vibrating, "that is splendid! It must have its effect, no matter what happens."

"Do you feel that?" he asked, taking a step toward her.

"Yes. When I see you, I feel it, I think." . . .

Whatever answer he might have made to this was frustrated by the appearance of the figure of Nelson Langmaid in the doorway. He seemed to survey them benevolently through his spectacles.

"How are you, Hodder? Well, Alison, I have to leave without seeing anything of you - you must induce your father not to bring his business home with him. Just a word," he added to the rector, "before you go up."

Hodder turned to Alison. "Good night," he said.

The gentle but unmistakable pressure of her hand he interpreted as the pinning on him of the badge of her faith. He was to go into battle wearing her colours. Their eyes met.

"Good night," she answered . . . .

In the hall the lawyer took his arm.

"What's the trouble, Hodder?" he asked, sympathetically.

Hodder, although on his guard, was somewhat taken aback by the directness of the onslaught.

"I'm afraid, Mr. Langmaid," the rector replied, "that it would take me longer to tell you than the time at your disposal."

Dear me," said the lawyer, "this is too bad. Why didn't you come to me? I am a good friend of yours, Hodder, and there is an additional bond between us on my sister's account. She is extremely fond of you, you know. And I have a certain feeling of responsibility for you, - I brought you here."

"You have always been very kind, and I appreciate it,"

Hodder replied. "I should be sorry to cause you any worry or annoyance. But you must understand that I cannot share the responsibility of my acts with any one."

"A little advice from an old legal head is sometimes not out of place. Even Dr. Gilman used to consult me. I hope you will bear in mind how remarkably well you have been getting along at St. John's, and what a success you've made."

"Success!" echoed the rector.

Either Mr. Langmaid read nothing in his face, or was determined to read nothing.

"Assuredly," he answered, benignly. "You have managed to please everybody, Mr. Parr included, - and some of us are not easy to please. I thought I'd tell you this, as a friend, as your first friend in the parish. Your achievement has been all the more remarkable, following, as you did, Dr. Gilman. Now it would greatly distress me to see that state of things disturbed, both for your sake and others. I thought I would just give you a hint, as you are going to see Mr. Parr, that he is in rather a nervous state. These so-called political reformers have upset the market and started a lot of legal complications that's why I'm here to-night. Go easy with him. I know you won't do anything foolish."

The lawyer accompanied this statement with a pat, but this time he did not succeed in concealing his concern.

"That depends on one's point of view," Hodder returned, with a smile. "I do not know how you have come to suspect that I am going to disturb Mr. Parr, but what I have to say to him is between him and me."

Langmaid took up his hat from the table, and sighed.

"Drop in on me sometime," he said, "I'd like to talk to you - Hodder heard a voice behind him, and turned. A servant was standing there.

"Mr. Parr is ready to see you, sir," he said.

The rector followed him up the stairs, to the room on the second floor, half office, half study, where the capitalist transacted his business when at home.

III

Eldon Parr was huddled over his desk reading a typewritten document; but he rose, and held out his hand, which Hodder took.

"How are you, Mr. Hodder? I'm sorry to have kept you waiting, but matters of some legal importance have arisen on which I was obliged to make a decision. You're well, I hope." He shot a glance at the rector, and sat down again, still holding the sheets. "If you will excuse me a moment longer, I'll finish this."

"Certainly," Hodder replied.

"Take a chair," said Mr. Parr, "you'll find the evening paper beside you."

Hodder sat down, and the banker resumed his perusal of the document, his eye running rapidly over the pages, pausing once in a while to scratch out a word or to make a note on the margin. In the concentration of the man on the task before him the rector read a design, an implication that the affairs of the Church were of a minor importance: sensed, indeed, the new attitude of hostility, gazed upon the undiscovered side, the dangerous side before which other men had quailed. Alison's words recurred to him, "they are afraid of you, they will crush you if they can." Eldon Parr betrayed, at any rate, no sign of fear. If his mental posture were further analyzed, it might be made out to contain an intimation that the rector, by some act, had forfeited the right to the unique privilege of the old relationship.

Well, the fact that the banker had, in some apparently occult manner, been warned, would make Hodder's task easier - or rather less difficult. His feelings were even more complicated than he had anticipated. The moments of suspense were trying to his nerves, and he had a shrewd notion that this making men wait was a favourite manoeuvre of Eldon Parr's; nor had he underrated the benumbing force of that personality. It was evident that the financier intended him to open the battle, and he was - as he had expected - finding it difficult to marshal the regiments of his arguments. In vain he thought of the tragedy of Garvin . . . . The thing was more complicated. And behind this redoubtable and sinister Eldon Parr he saw, as it were, the wraith of that: other who had once confessed the misery of his loneliness. . . .

At last the banker rang, sharply, the bell on his desk. A secretary entered, to whom he dictated a telegram which contained these words: "Langmaid has discovered a way out." It was to be sent to an address in Texas. Then he turned in his chair and crossed his knees, his hand fondling an ivory paper-cutter. He smiled a little.

"Well, Mr. Hodder," he said.

The rector, intensely on his guard, merely inclined his head in recognition that his turn had come.

"I was sorry," the banker continued, after a perceptible pause, - that you could not see your way clear to have come with me on the cruise."

"I must thank you again," Hodder answered, "but I felt - as I wrote you - that certain matters made it impossible for me to go."

"I suppose you had your reasons, but I think you would have enjoyed the trip. I had a good, seaworthy boat - I chartered her from Mr. Lieber, the president of the Continental Zinc, you know. I went as far as Labrador. A wonderful coast, Mr. Hodder."

"It must be," agreed the rector. It was clear that Mr. Parr intended to throw upon him the onus of the first move. There was a silence, brief, indeed, but long enough for Hodder to feel more and more distinctly the granite hardness which the other had become, to experience a rising, reenforcing anger. He went forward, steadily but resolutely, on the crest of it. "I have remained in the city," he continued, "and I have had the opportunity to discover certain facts of which I have hitherto been ignorant, and which, in my opinion, profoundly affect the welfare of the church. It is of these I wished to speak to you."

Mr. Parr waited.

"It is not much of an exaggeration to say that ever since I came here I have been aware that St. John's, considering the long standing of the parish, the situation of the church in a thickly populated district, is not fulfilling its mission. But I have failed until now to perceive the causes of that inefficiency."

"Inefficiency?" The banker repeated the word.

"Inefficiency," said Hodder. "The reproach, the responsibility is largely mine, as the rector, the spiritual, head of the parish. I believe I am right when I say that the reason for the decision, some twenty years ago, to leave the church where it is, instead of selling the property and building in the West End, was that it might minister to the poor in the neighbourhood, to bring religion and hope into their lives, and to exert its influence towards eradicating the vice and misery which surround it."

"But I thought you had agreed," said Mr. Parr, coldly, "that we were to provide for that in the new chapel and settlement house."

"For reasons which I hope to make plain to you, Mr. Parr," Hodder replied, "those people can never be reached, as they ought to be reached, by building that settlement house. The principle is wrong, the day is past when such things can be done - in that way." He laid an emphasis on these words. "It is good, I grant you, to care for the babies and children of the poor, it is good to get young women and men out of the dance-halls, to provide innocent amusement, distraction, instruction. But it is not enough. It leaves the great, transforming thing in the lives of these people untouched, and it will forever remain untouched so long as a sense of wrong, a continually deepening impression of an unchristian civilization upheld by the Church herself, exists. Such an undertaking as that settlement house - I see clearly now - is a palliation, a poultice applied to one of many sores, a compromise unworthy of the high mission of the Church. She should go to the root of the disease. It is her first business to make Christians, who, by amending their own lives, by going out individually and collectively into the life of the nation, will gradually remove these conditions."

Mr. Parr sat drumming on the table. Hodder met

his look.

"So you, too, have come to it," he said.

"Have come to what?"

"Socialism."

Hodder, in the state of clairvoyance in which he now surprisingly found himself, accurately summed up the value and meaning of the banker's sigh.

"Say, rather," he replied, "that I have come to Christianity. We shall never have what is called socialism until there is no longer any necessity for it, until men, of their owe free will, are ready to renounce selfish, personal ambition and power and work for humanity, for the state."

Mr. Parr's gesture implied that he cared not by what name the thing was called, but he still appeared strangely, astonishingly calm; - Hodder, with all his faculties acute, apprehended that he was dangerously calm. The man who had formerly been his friend was now completely obliterated, and he had the feeling almost of being about to grapple, in mortal combat, with some unknown monster whose tactics and resources were infinite, whose victims had never escaped. The monster was in Eldon Parr - that is how it came to him. The waxy, relentless demon was aroused. It behooved him, Hodder, to step carefully . . . .

"That is all very fine, Mr. Hodder, very altruistic, very Christian, I've no doubt-but the world doesn't work that way." (These were the words borne in on Hodder's consciousness.) "What drives the world is the motive furnished by the right of acquiring and holding property. If we had a division to-day, the able men would come out on top next year."

The rector shook his head. He remembered, at that moment, Horace Bentley.

"What drives the world is a far higher motive, Mr. Parr, the motive with which have been fired the great lights of history, the motive of renunciation and service which is transforming governments, which is gradually making the world a better place in which to live. And we are seeing men and women imbued with it, rising in ever increasing numbers on every side to-day."

"Service!" Eldon Parr had seized upon the word as it passed and held it. "What do you think my life has been? I suppose," he said, with a touch of intense bitterness, "that you, too, who six months ago seemed as reasonable a man as I ever met, have joined in the chorus of denunciators. It has become the fashion to-day, thanks to your socialists, reformers, and agitators, to decry a man because he is rich, to take it for granted that he is a thief and a scoundrel, that he has no sense of responsibility for his country and his fellow-men. The glory, the true democracy of this nation, lies in its equal opportunity for all. They take no account of that, of the fact that each has had the same chance as his fellows. No, but they cry out that the man who, by the sweat of his brow, has earned wealth ought to divide it up with the lazy and the self-indulgent and the shiftless.

"Take my case, for instance, - it is typical of thousands. I came to this city as a boy in my teens, with eight dollars in my pocket which I had earned on a farm. I swept the floor, cleaned the steps, moved boxes and ran errands in Gabriel Parker's store on Third Street. I was industrious, sober, willing to do anything. I fought, I tell you every inch of my way. As soon as I saved a little money I learned to use every ounce of brain I possessed to hold on to it. I trusted a man once, and I had to begin all over again. And I discovered, once for all, if a man doesn't look out for himself, no one will.

"I don't pretend that I am any better than any one else, I have had to take life as I found it, and make the best of it. I conformed to the rules of the game; I soon had sense enough knocked into me to understand that the conditions were not of my making. But I'll say this for myself," Eldon Parr leaned forward over the blotter, "I had standards, and I stuck by them. I wanted to be a decent citizen, to bring up my children in the right way. I didn't squander my money, when I got it, on wine and women, I respected other men's wives, I supported the Church and the institutions of the city. I too even I had my ambitions, my ideals - and they were not entirely worldly ones. You would probably accuse me of wishing to acquire only the position of power which I hold. If you had accepted my invitation to go aboard the yacht this summer, it was my intention to unfold to you a scheme of charities which has long been forming in my mind, and which I think would be of no small benefit to the city where I have made my fortune. I merely mention this to prove to you that I am not unmindful, in spite of the circumstances of my own life, of the unfortunates whose mental equipment is not equal to my own."

By this "poor boy" argument which - if Hodder had known - Mr. Parr had used at banquets with telling effect, the banker seemed to regain perspective and equilibrium, to plant his feet once more on the rock of the justification of his life, and from which, by a somewhat extraordinary process he had not quite understood, he had been partially shaken off. As he had proceeded with his personal history, his manner had gradually become one of the finality of experience over theory, of the forbearance of the practical man with the visionary. Like most successful citizens of his type, he possessed in a high degree the faculty of creating sympathy, of compelling others to accept - temporarily, at least - his point of view. It was this faculty, Hodder perceived, which had heretofore laid an enchantment upon him, and it was not without a certain wonder that he now felt himself to be released from the spell.

The perceptions of the banker were as keen, and his sense of security was brief. Somehow, as he met the searching eye of the rector, he was unable to see the man as a visionary, but beheld - and, to do him justice - felt a twinge of respect for an adversary worthy of his steel.

He, who was accustomed to prepare for clouds when they were mere specks on his horizon, paused even now to marvel why he had not dealt with this. Here was a man - a fanatic, if he liked - but still a man who positively did not fear him, to whom his wrath and power were as nothing! A new and startling and complicated sensation - but Eldon Parr was no coward. If he had, consciously or unconsciously, formerly looked upon the clergyman as a dependent, Hodder appeared to be one no more. The very ruggedness of the man had enhanced, expanded - as it were - until it filled the room. And Hodder had, with an audacity unparalleled in the banker's experience arraigned by implication his whole life, managed to put him on the defensive.

"But if that be your experience," the rector said, "and it has become your philosophy, what is it in you that impels you to give these large sums for the public good?"

"I should suppose that you, as a clergyman, might understand that my motive is a Christian one."

Hodder sat very still, but a higher light came into his eyes.

"Mr. Parr," he replied, "I have been a friend of yours, and I am a friend still. And what I am going to tell you is not only in the hope that others may benefit, but that your own soul may be saved. I mean that literally - your own soul. You are under the impression that you are a Christian, but you are not and never have been one. And you will not be one until your whole life is transformed, until you become a different man. If you do not change, it is my duty to warn you that the sorrow and suffering, the uneasiness which you now know, and which drive you on, in search of distraction, to adding useless sums of money to your fortune - this suffering, I say, will become intensified. You will die in the knowledge of it, and live on after, in the knowledge of it."

In spite of himself, the financier drew back before this unexpected blast, the very intensity of which had struck a chill of terror in his inmost being. He had been taken off his guard, - for he had supposed the day long past - if it had ever existed - when a spiritual rebuke would upset him; the day long past when a minister could pronounce one with any force. That the Church should ever again presume to take herself seriously had never occurred to him. And yet - the man had denounced him in a moment of depression, of nervous irritation and exasperation against a government which had begun to interfere with the sacred liberty of its citizens, against political agitators who had spurred that government on. The world was mad. No element, it seemed, was now content to remain in its proper place. His voice, as he answered, shook with rage, - all the greater because the undaunted sternness by which it was confronted seemed to reduce it to futility.

"Take care!" he cried, "take care! You, nor any other man, clergyman or no clergyman, have any right to be the judge of my conduct."

"On the contrary," said Holder, "if your conduct affects the welfare, the progress, the reputation of the church of which I am rector, I have the right. And I intend to exercise it. It becomes my duty, however painful, to tell you, as a member of the Church, wherein you have wronged the Church and wronged yourself."

He didn't raise his tone, and there was in it more of sorrow than of indignation. The banker turned an ashen gray . . A moment elapsed before he spoke, a transforming moment. He suddenly became ice.

"Very well," he said. "I can't pretend to account for these astounding views you have acquired - and I am using a mild term. Let me say this: (he leaned forward a little, across the desk) I demand that you be specific. I am a busy man, I have little time to waste, I have certain matters - before me which must be attended to to-night. I warn you that I will not listen any longer to vague accusations."

It was Holder's turn to marvel. Did Eldon Purr, after all; have no sense of guilt? Instantaneously, automatically, his own anger rose.

"You may be sure, Mr. Parr, that I should not be here unless I were prepared to be specific. And what I am going to say to you I have reserved for your ear alone, in the hope that you will take it to heart, while it is not yet too late, said amend your life accordingly."

Eldon Parr shifted slightly. His look became inscrutable, was riveted on the rector.

"I shall call your attention first to a man of whom you have probably never heard. He is dead now - he threw himself into the river this summer, with a curse on his lips - I am afraid - a curse against you. A few years ago he lived happily with his wife and child in a little house on the Grade Suburban, and he had several thousand dollars as a result of careful saving and systematic self-denial.

"Perhaps you have never thought of the responsibilities of a great name. This man, like thousands of others in the city, idealized you. He looked up to you as the soul of honour, as a self-made man who by his own unaided efforts - as you yourself have just pointed out - rose from a poor boy to a position of power and trust in the community. He saw you a prominent layman in the Church of God. He was dazzled by the brilliancy of your success, inspired by a civilization which - gave such opportunities. He recognized that he himself had not the brains for such an achievement, - his hope and love and ambition were centred in his boy."

At the word Eldon Parr's glance was suddenly dulled by pain. He tightened his lips.

"That boy was then of a happy, merry disposition, so the mother says, and every summer night as she cooked supper she used to hear him laughing as he romped in the yard with his father. When I first saw him this summer, it was two days before his father committed suicide. The child was lying, stifled with the heat, in the back room of one of those desolate lodging houses in Dalton Street, and his little body had almost wasted away.

"While I was there the father came in, and when he saw me he was filled with fury. He despised the Church, and St. John's above all churches, because you were of it; because you who had given so generously to it had wrecked his life. You had shattered his faith in humanity, his ideal. From a normal, contented man he had deteriorated into a monomaniac whom no one would hire, a physical and mental wreck who needed care and nursing. He said he hoped the boy would die.

"And what had happened? The man had bought, with all the money he had in the world, Consolidated Tractions. He had bought it solely because of his admiration for your ability, his faith in your name. It was inconceivable to him that a man of your standing, a public benefactor, a supporter of church and charities, would permit your name to be connected with any enterprise that was not sound and just. Thousands like Garvin lost all they had, while you are still a rich man. It is further asserted that you sold out all your stock at a high price, with the exception of that in the leased lines, which are guaranteed heavy dividends."

"Have you finished?" demanded Eldon Parr.

"Not quite, on this subject," replied the rector. "Two nights after that, the man threw himself in the river. His body was pulled out by men on a tugboat, and his worthless stock certificate was in his pocket. It is now in the possession of Mr. Horace Bentley. Thanks to Mr. Bentley, the widow found a temporary home, and the child has almost recovered."

Hodder paused. His interest had suddenly become concentrated upon the banker's new demeanour, and he would not have thought it within the range of possibility that a man could listen to such a revelation concerning himself without the betrayal of some feeling. But so it was, - Eldon Parr had been coldly attentive, save for the one scarcely perceptible tremor when the boy was mentioned. His interrogatory gesture gave the very touch of perfection to this attitude, since it proclaimed him to have listened patiently to a charge so preposterous that a less reasonable man would have cut it short.

"And what leads you to suppose," he inquired, "that I am responsible in this matter? What leads you to infer that the Consolidated Tractions Company was not organized in good faith? Do you think that business men are always infallible? The street-car lines of this city were at sixes and sevens, fighting each other; money was being wasted by poor management. The idea behind the company was a public-spirited one, to give the citizens cheaper and better service, by a more modern equipment, by a wider system of transfer. It seems to me, Mr. Hodder, that you put yourself in a more quixotic position than the so-called reformers when you assume that the men who organize a company in good faith are personally responsible for every share of stock that is sold, and for the welfare of every individual who may buy the stock. We force no one to buy it. They do so at their own risk. I myself have thousands of dollars of worthless stock in my safe. I have never complained."

The full force of Hodder's indignation went into his reply.

"I am not talking about the imperfect code of human justice under which we live, Mr. Parr," he cried. "This is not a case in which a court of law may exonerate you, it is between you and your God. But I have taken the trouble to find out, from unquestioned sources, the truth about the Consolidated Tractions Company - I shall not go into the details at length - they are doubtless familiar to you. I know that the legal genius of Mr. Langmaid, one of my vestry, made possible the organization of the company, and thereby evaded the plain spirit of the law of the state. I know that one branch line was bought for two hundred and fifty thousand dollars, and capitalized for three millions, and that most of the others were scandalously over-capitalized. I know that while the coming transaction was still a secret, you and other, gentlemen connected with the matter bought up large interests in other lines, which you proceeded to lease to yourselves at guaranteed dividends which these lines do not earn. I know that the first large dividend was paid out of capital. And the stock which you sold to poor Garvin was so hopelessly watered that it never could have been anything but worthless. If, in spite of these facts, you do not deem yourself responsible for the misery which has been caused, if your conscience is now clear, it is my duty to tell you that there is a higher bar of justice."

The intensity of the fire of the denunciation had, indeed, a momentary yet visible effect in the banker's expression. Whatever the emotions thus lashed to self-betrayal, anger, hatred, - fear, perhaps, Hodder could not detect a trace of penitence; and he was aware, on the part of the other, of a supreme, almost spasmodic effort for self-control. The constitutional reluctance of Eldon Parr to fight openly could not have been more clearly demonstrated.

"Because you are a clergyman, Mr. Hodder," he began, "because you are the rector of St. John's, I have allowed you to say things to me which I would not have permitted from any other man. I have tried to take into account your point of view, which is naturally restricted, your pardonable ignorance of what business men, who wish to do their duty by Church and State, have to contend with. When you came to this parish you seemed to have a sensible, a proportional view of things; you were content to confine your activities to your own sphere, content not to meddle with politics and business, which you could, at first hand, know nothing about. The modern desire of clergymen to interfere in these matters has ruined the usefulness of many of them.

"I repeat, I have tried to be patient. I venture to hope, still, that this extraordinary change in you may not be permanent, but merely the result of a natural sympathy with the weak and unwise and unfortunate who are always to be found in a complex civilization. I can even conceive how such a discovery must have shocked you, temporarily aroused your indignation, as a clergyman, against the world as it is - and, I may add, as it has always been. My personal friendship for you, and my interest in your future welfare impel me to make a final appeal to you not to ruin a career which is full of promise."

The rector did not take advantage of the pause. A purely psychological curiosity hypnotized him to see how far the banker would go in his apparent generosity.

"I once heard you say, I believe, in a sermon, that the Christian religion is a leaven. It is the leaven that softens and ameliorates the hard conditions of life, that makes our relations with our fellow-men bearable. But life is a contest, it is war. It always has been, and always will be. Business is war, commerce is war, both among nations and individuals. You cannot get around it. If a man does not exterminate his rivals they will exterminate him. In other days churches were built and endowed with the spoils of war, and did not disdain the money. To-day they cheerfully accept the support and gifts of business men. I do not accuse them of hypocrisy. It is a recognition on their part that business men, in spite of hard facts, are not unmindful of the spiritual side of life, and are not deaf to the injunction to help others. And when, let me ask you, could you find in the world's history more splendid charities than are around us to-day? Institutions endowed for medical research, for the conquest of deadly diseases? libraries, hospitals, schools - men giving their fortunes for these things, the fruits of a life's work so laboriously acquired? Who can say that the modern capitalist is not liberal, is not a public benefactor?

"I dislike being personal, but you have forced it upon me. I dislike to refer to what I have already done in the matter of charities, but I hinted to you awhile ago of a project I have conceived and almost perfected of gifts on a much larger scale than I have ever attempted." The financier stared at him meaningly. "And I had you in mind as one of the three men whom I should consult, whom I should associate with myself in the matter. We cannot change human nature, but we can better conditions by wise giving. I do not refer now to the settle ment house, which I am ready to help make and maintain as the best in the country, but I have in mind a system to be carried out with the consent and aid of the municipal government, of play-grounds, baths, parks, places of recreation, and hospitals, for the benefit of the people, which will put our city in the very forefront of progress. And I believe, as a practical man, I can convince you that the betterment which you and I so earnestly desire can be brought about in no other way. Agitation can only result in anarchy and misery for all."

Hodder's wrath, as he rose from his chair, was of the sort that appears incredibly to add to the physical stature, - the bewildering spiritual wrath which is rare indeed, and carries all before it.

"Don't tempt me, Mr. Parr!" he said. "Now that I know the truth, I tell you frankly I would face poverty and persecution rather than consent to your offer. And I warn you once more not to flatter yourself that existence ends here, that you will, not be called to answer for every wrong act you have committed in accumulating your fortune, that what you call business is an affair of which God takes no account. What I say may seem foolishness to you, but I tell you, in the words of that Foolishness, that it will not profit you to gain the whole world and lose your own soul. You remind me that the Church in old time accepted gifts from the spoils of war, and I will add of rapine and murder. And the Church to-day, to repeat your own parallel, grows rich with money wrongfully got. Legally? Ah, yes, legally, perhaps. But that will not avail you. And the kind of church you speak of - to which I, to my shame, once consented - Our Lord repudiates. It is none of his. I warn you, Mr. Parr, in his Name, first to make your peace with your brothers before you presume to lay another gift on the altar."

During this withering condemnation of himself Eldon Parr sat motionless, his face grown livid, an expression on it that continued to haunt Hodder long afterwards. An expression, indeed, which made the banker almost unrecognizable.

"Go, he whispered, his hand trembling visibly as he pointed towards the door. "Go - I have had enough of this."

"Not until I have said one thing more," replied the rector, undaunted. "I have found the woman whose marriage with your son you prevented, whom you bought off and started on the road to hell without any sense of responsibility. You have made of her a prostitute and a drunkard. Whether she can be rescued or not is problematical. She, too, is in Mr. Bentley's care, a man upon whom you once showed no mercy. I leave Garvin, who has gone to his death, and Kate Marcy and Horace Bentley to your conscience, Mr. Parr. That they are representative of many others, I do not doubt. I tell you solemnly that the whole meaning of life is service to others, and I warn you, before it is too late, to repent and make amends. Gifts will not help you, and charities are of no avail."

At the reference to Kate Marcy Eldon Parr's hand dropped to his side. He seemed to have physical difficulty in speaking.

"Ah, you have found that woman!" He leaned an elbow on the desk, he seemed suddenly to have become weary, spent, old. And Hodder, as he watched him, perceived - that his haggard look was directed towards a photograph in a silver frame on the table - a photograph of Preston Parr. At length he broke the silence.

"What would you have had me do?" he asked. "Permit my son to marry a woman of the streets, I suppose. That would have been Christianity, according to your notion. Come now, what world you have done, if your son had been in question?"

A wave of pity swept over the rector.

"Why," he said, why did you have nothing but cruelty in your heart, and contempt for her? When you saw that she was willing, for the love of the son whom you loved, to give up all that life meant to her, how could you destroy her without a qualm? The crime you committed was that you refused to see God in that woman's soul, when he had revealed himself to you. You looked for wile, for cunning, for self-seeking, - and they were not there. Love had obliterated them. When you saw how meekly she obeyed you, and agreed to go away, why did you not have pity? If you had listened to your conscience, you would have known what to do.

"I do not say that you should not have opposed the marriage - then. Marriage is not to be lightly entered into. From the moment you went to see her you became responsible for her. You hurled her into the abyss, and she has come back to haunt you. You should have had her educated and cared for - she would have submitted, to any plan you proposed. And if, after a sensible separation, you became satisfied as to her character and development, and your son still wished to marry her, you should have withdrawn your objections.

"As it is, and in consequence of your act, you have lost your son. He left you then, and you have no more control over him."

"Stop!" cried Eldon Parr, "for God's sake stop! I won't stand any more of this. I will not listen to criticism of my life, to strictures on my conduct from you or any other man." He reached for a book on the corner of his desk - a cheque book. - "You'll want money for these people, I suppose," he added brutally. "I will give it, but it must be understood that I do not recognize any right of theirs to demand it."

For a moment Holder did not trust himself to reply. He looked down across the desk at the financier, who was fumbling with the leaves.

"They do not demand it, Mr. Parr," he answered, gently. "And I have tried to make it plain to you that you have lost the right to give it. I expected to fail in this. I have failed."

"What do you mean?" Eldon Parr let the cheque book close.

"I mean what I said," the rector replied. "That if you would save your soul you must put an end, to-morrow, to the acquisition of money, and devote the rest of your life to an earnest and sincere attempt to make just restitution to those you have wronged. And you must ask the forgiveness of God for your sins. Until you do that, your charities are abominations in his sight. I will not trouble you any longer, except to say that I shall be ready to come to you at any time my presence may be of any help to you."

The banker did not speak . . . . With a single glance towards the library Holder left the house, but paused for a moment outside to gaze back at it, as it loomed in the darkness against the stars.

CHAPTER XXI

ALISON GOES TO CHURCH

I

On the following Sunday morning the early light filtered into Alison's room, and she opened her strong eyes. Presently she sprang from her bed and drew back the curtains of the windows, gazing rapturously into the crystal day. The verdure of the Park was freshened to an incredible brilliancy by the dew, a thin white veil of mist was spread over the mirror of the waters, the trees flung long shadows across the turf.

A few minutes later she was out, thrilled by the silence, drawing in deep, breaths of the morning air; lingering by still lakes catching the blue of the sky - a blue that left its stain upon the soul; as the sun mounted she wandered farther, losing herself in the wilderness of the forest.

At eight o'clock, when she returned, there were signs that the city had awakened. A mounted policeman trotted past her as she crossed a gravel drive, and on the tree-flecked stretches, which lately had been empty as Eden, human figures were scattered. A child, with a sailboat that languished for lack of wind, stared at her, first with fascination and wonder in his eyes, and then smiled at her tentatively. She returned the smile with a start.

Children had stared at her like that before now, and for the first time in her life she asked herself what the look might mean. She had never really been fond of them: she had never, indeed, been brought much in contact with them. But now, without warning, a sudden fierce yearning took possession of her: surprised and almost frightened, she stopped irresistibly and looked back at the thin little figure crouched beside the water, to discover that his widened eyes were still upon her. Her own lingered on him shyly, and thus for a moment she hung in doubt whether to flee or stay, her heart throbbing as though she were on the brink of some unknown and momentous adventure. She took a timid step.

"What's your name?" she asked.

The boy told her.

"What's yours?" he ventured, still under the charm.

"Alison."

He had never heard of that name, and said so. They deplored the lack of wind. And presently, still mystified, but gathering courage, he asked her why she blushed, at which her colour deepened.

"I can't help it," she told him.

"I like it," the boy said.

Though the grass was still wet, she got down on her

knees in her white skirt, the better to push the boat along the shore: once it drifted beyond their reach, and was only rescued by a fallen branch discovered with difficulty.

The arrival of the boy's father, an anaemic-looking little man, put an end to their play. He deplored the condition of the lady's dress.

"It doesn't matter in the least," she assured him, and fled in a mood she did not attempt to analyze. Hurrying homeward, she regained her room, bathed, and at half past eight appeared in the big, formal dining-room, from which the glare of the morning light was carefully screened. Her father insisted on breakfasting here; and she found him now seated before the white table-cloth, reading a newspaper. He glanced up at her critically.

"So you've decided to honour me this morning," he said.

"I've been out in the Park," she replied, taking the chair opposite him. He resumed his reading, but presently, as she was pouring out the coffee, he lowered the paper again.

"What's the occasion to-day?" he asked.

"The occasion?" she repeated, without acknowledging that she had instantly grasped his implication. His eyes were on her gown.

"You are not accustomed, as a rule, to pay much deference to Sunday."

"Doesn't the Bible say, somewhere," she inquired, "that the Sabbath was made for man? Perhaps that may be broadened after a while, to include woman."

"But you have never been an advocate, so far as I know, of women taking advantage of their opportunity by going to Church."

"What's the use," demanded Alison, "of the thousands of working women spending the best part of the day in the ordinary church, when their feet and hands and heads are aching? Unless some fire is kindled in their souls, it is hopeless for them to try to obtain any benefit from religion - so-called - as it is preached to them in most churches."

"Fire in their souls!" exclaimed the banker.

"Yes. If the churches offered those who might be leaders among their fellows a practical solution of existence, kindled their self-respect, replaced a life of drudgery by one of inspiration - that would be worth while. But you will never get such a condition as that unless your pulpits are filled by personalities, instead of puppets who are all cast in one mould, and who profess to be there by divine right."

"I am glad to see at least that you are taking an interest in religious matters," her father observed, meaningly.

Alison coloured. But she retorted with spirit.

"That is true of a great many persons to-day who are thinking on the subject. If Christianity is a solution of life, people are demanding of the churches that they shall perform their function, and show us how, and why, or else cease to encumber the world."

Eldon Parr folded up his newspaper.

"So you are going to Church this morning," he said.

"Yes. At what time will you be ready?"

"At quarter to eleven. But if you are going to St. John', you will have to start earlier. I'll order a car at half past ten."

"Where are you going?" She held her breath, unconsciously, for the answer.

"To Calvary," he replied coldly, as he rose to leave the room. "But I hesitate to ask you to come, - I am afraid you will not find a religion there that suits you."

For a moment she could not trust herself to speak. The secret which, ever since Friday evening, she had been burning to learn was disclosed . . . Her father had broken with Mr. Hodder!

"Please don't order the motor for me," she said. "I'd rather go in the street cars."

She sat very still in the empty room, her face burning.

Characteristically, her father had not once mentioned the rector of St. John's, yet had contrived to imply that her interest in Hodder was greater than her interest in religion. And she was forced to admit, with her customary honesty, that the implication was true.

The numbers who knew Alison Parr casually thought

her cold. They admired a certain quality in her work, but they did not suspect that that quality was the incomplete expression of an innate idealism capable of being fanned into flame, - for she was subject to rare but ardent enthusiasms which kindled and transformed her incredibly in the eyes of the few to whom the process had been revealed. She had had even a longer list of suitors than any one guessed; men who - usually by accident - had touched the hidden spring, and suddenly beholding an unimagined woman, had consequently lost their heads. The mistake most of them had made (for subtlety in such affairs is not a masculine trait) was the failure to recognize and continue to present the quality in them which had awakened her. She had invariably discovered the feet of clay.

Thus disillusion had been her misfortune - perhaps it would be more accurate to say her fortune. She had built up, after each invasion, her defences more carefully and solidly than before, only to be again astonished and dismayed by the next onslaught, until at length the question had become insistent - the question of an alliance for purposes of greater security. She had returned to her childhood home to consider it, frankly recognizing it as a compromise, a fall . . . .

And here, in this sanctuary of her reflection, and out of a quarter on which she had set no watch, out of a wilderness which she had believed to hold nothing save the ruined splendours of the past, had come one who, like the traditional figures of the wilderness, had attracted her by his very uncouthness and latent power. And the anomaly he presented in what might be called the vehemence of his advocacy of an outworn orthodoxy, in his occupation of the pulpit of St. John's, had quickened at once her curiosity and antagonism. It had been her sudden discovery, or rather her instinctive suspicion of the inner conflict in him which had set her standard fluttering in response. Once more (for the last time - something whispered - now) she had become the lady of the lists; she sat on her walls watching, with beating heart and straining eyes, the closed helm of her champion, ready to fling down the revived remnant of her faith as prize or forfeit. She had staked all on the hope that he would not lower his lance. . . . .

Saturday had passed in suspense . . . . And now was flooding in on her the certainty that he had not failed her; that he had, with a sublime indifference to a worldly future and success, defied the powers. With indifference, too, to her! She knew, of course, that he loved her. A man with less of greatness would have sought a middle way . . . .

When, at half past ten, she fared forth into the sunlight, she was filled with anticipation, excitement, concern, feelings enhanced and not soothed by the pulsing vibrations of the church bells in the softening air. The swift motion of the electric car was grateful. . . But at length the sight of familiar landmarks, old-fashioned dwellings crowded in between the stores and factories of lower Tower Street, brought back recollections of the days when she had come this way, other Sunday mornings, and in a more leisurely public vehicle, with her mother. Was it possible that she, Alison Parr, were going to church now? Her excitement deepened, and she found it difficult to bring herself to the realization that her destination was a church - the church of her childhood. At this moment she could only think of St. John's as the setting of the supreme drama.

When she alighted at the corner of Burton Street there was the well-remembered, shifting group on the pavement in front of the church porch. How many times, in the summer and winter, in fair weather and cloudy, in rain and sleet and snow had she approached that group, as she approached it now! Here were the people, still, in the midst of whom her earliest associations had been formed, changed, indeed,-but yet the same. No, the change was in her, and the very vastness of that change came as a shock. These had stood still, anchored to their traditions, while she - had she grown? or merely wandered? She had searched, at least, and seen. She had once accepted them - if indeed as a child it could have been said of her that she accepted anything; she had been unable then, at any rate, to bring forward any comparisons.

Now she beheld them, collectively, in their complacent finery, as representing a force, a section of the army blocking the heads of the passes of the world's progress, resting on their arms, but ready at the least uneasy movement from below to man the breastworks, to fling down the traitor from above, to fight fiercely for the solidarity of their order. And Alison even believed herself to detect, by something indefinable in their attitudes as they stood momentarily conversing in lowered voices, an aroused suspicion, an uneasy anticipation. Her imagination went so far as to apprehend, as they greeted her unwonted appearance, that they read in it an addition to other vague and disturbing phenomena. Her colour was high.

"Why, my dear," said Mrs. Atterbury, "I thought you had gone back to New York long ago!"

Beside his mother stood Gordon - more dried up, it

seemed, than ever. Alison recalled him, as on this very spot, a thin, pale boy in short trousers, and Mrs. Atterbury a beautiful and controlled young matron associated with St. John's and with children's parties. She was wonderful yet, with her white hair and straight nose, her erect figure still slight. Alison knew that Mrs. Atterbury had never forgiven her for rejecting her son - or rather for being the kind of woman who could reject him.

"Surely you haven't been here all summer?"

Alison admitted it, characteristically, without explanations.

"It seems so natural to see you here at the old church, after all these years," the lady went on, and Alison was aware that Mrs. Atterbury questioned - or rather was at a loss for the motives which had led such an apostate back to the fold. "We must thank Mr. Hodder, I suppose. He's very remarkable. I hear he is resuming the services to-day for the first time since June."

Alison was inclined to read a significance into Mrs. Atterbury's glance at her son, who was clearing his throat.

"But - where is Mr. Parr?" he asked. "I understand he has come back from his cruise."

"Yes, he is back. I came without - him - -as you see."

She found a certain satisfaction in adding to the mystification, to the disquietude he betrayed by fidgeting more than usual.

"But - he always comes when he is in town. Business - I suppose - ahem!"

"No," replied Alison, dropping her bomb with cruel precision, "he has gone to Calvary."

The agitation was instantaneous.

"To Calvary!" exclaimed mother and son in one breath.

"Why?" It was Gordon who demanded. "A - a special occasion there - a bishop or something?"

"I'm afraid you must ask him," she said.

She was delayed on the steps, first by Nan Ferguson, then by the Laureston Greys, and her news outdistanced her to the porch. Charlotte Plimpton looking very red and solid, her eyes glittering with excitement, blocked her way.

"Alison?" she cried, in the slightly nasal voice that was a Gore inheritance, "I'm told your father's gone to Calvary! Has Mr. Hodder offended him? I heard rumours - Wallis seems to be afraid that something has happened."

"He hasn't said anything about it to me, Charlotte," said Alison, in quiet amusement," but then he wouldn't, you know. I don't live here any longer, and he has no reason to think that I would be interested in church matters."

"But - why did you come?" Charlotte demanded, with Gore naivete.

Alison smiled.

"You mean - what was my motive?"

Charlotte actually performed the miracle of getting redder. She was afraid of Alison - much more afraid since she had known of her vogue in the East. When Alison had put into execution the astounding folly (to the Gore mind) of rejecting the inheritance of millions to espouse a profession, it had been Charlotte Plimpton who led the chorus of ridicule and disapproval. But success, to the Charlotte Plimptons, is its own justification, and now her ambition (which had ramifications) was to have Alison "do" her a garden. Incidentally, the question had flashed through her mind as to how much Alison's good looks had helped towards her triumph in certain shining circles.

"Oh, of course I didn't mean that," she hastened to deny, although it was exactly what she had meant. Her curiosity unsatisfied - and not likely to be satisfied at once, she shifted abruptly to the other burning subject. "I was so glad when I learned you hadn't gone. Grace Larrabbee's garden is a dream, my dear. Wallis and I stopped there the other day and the caretaker showed it to us. Can't you make a plan for me, so that I may begin next spring? And there's something else I wanted to ask you. Wallis and I are going to New York the end of the month. Shall you be there?"

"I don't know," said Alison, cautiously.

"We want so much to see one or two of your gardens on Long Island, and especially the Sibleys', on the Hudson. I know it will be late in the season, - but don't you think you could take us, Alison? And I intend to give you a dinner. I'll write you a note. Here's Wallis."

"Well, well, well," said Mr. Plimpton, shaking Alison's hand. "Where's father? I hear he's gone to Calvary."

Alison made her escape. Inside the silent church, Eleanor Goodrich gave her a smile and a pressure of welcome. Beside her, standing behind the rear pew, were Asa Waring and - Mr. Bentley! Mr. Bentley returned to St. John's!

"You have come!" Alison whispered.

He understood her. He took her hand in his and looked down into her upturned face.

"Yes, my dear," he said, "and my girls have come Sally Grover and the others, and some friends from Dalton Street and elsewhere."

The news, the sound of this old gentleman's voice and the touch of his hand suddenly filled her with a strange yet sober happiness. Asa Waring, though he had not overheard, smiled at her too, as in sympathy. His austere face was curiously illuminated, and she knew instinctively that in some way he shared her happiness. Mr. Bentley had come back! Yes, it was an augury. From childhood she had always admired Asa Waring, and now she felt a closer tie . . . .

She reached the pew, hesitated an instant, and slipped forward on her knees. Years had gone by since she had prayed, and even now she made no attempt to translate into words the intensity of her yearning - for what? Hodder's success, for one thing, - and by success she meant that he might pursue an unfaltering course. True to her temperament, she did not look for the downfall of the forces opposed to him. She beheld him persecuted, yet unyielding, and was thus lifted to an exaltation that amazed. . . If he could do it, such a struggle must sorely have an ultimate meaning! Thus she found herself, trembling, on the borderland of faith. . .

She arose, bewildered, her pulses beating. And presently glancing about, she took in that the church was fuller than she ever remembered having seen it, and the palpitating suspense she felt seemed to pervade, as it were, the very silence. With startling abruptness, the silence was broken by the tones of the great organ that rolled and reverberated among the arches; distant voices took up the processional; the white choir filed past, - first the treble voices of the boys, then the deeper notes of the - men, - turned and mounted the chancel steps, and then she saw Hodder. Her pew being among the first, he passed very near her. Did he know she would be there? The sternness of his profile told her nothing. He seemed at that moment removed, set apart, consecrated - this was the word that came to her, and yet she was keenly conscious of his presence.

Tingling, she found herself repeating, inwardly, two, lines of the hymn

> "Lay hold on life, and it shall be
> Thy joy and crown eternally."

"Lay hold on life!"

The service began, - the well-remembered, beautiful appeal and prayers which she could still repeat, after a lapse of time, almost by heart; and their music and rhythm, the simple yet magnificent language in which. they were clothed - her own language - awoke this morning a racial instinct strong in her, - she had not known how strong. Or was it something in Hodder's voice that seemed to illumine the ancient words with a new meaning? Raising her eyes to the chancel she studied his head, and found in it still another expression of that race, the history of which had been one of protest, of development of its own character and personality. Her mind went back to her first talk with him, in the garden, and she saw how her intuition had recognized in him then the spirit of a people striving to assert itself.

She stood with tightened lips, during the Apostles' Creed, listening to his voice as it rose, strong and unfaltering, above the murmur of the congregation.

At last she saw him swiftly crossing the chancel, mounting the pulpit steps, and he towered above her, a dominant figure, his white surplice sharply outlined against the dark stone of the pillar. The hymn died away, the congregation sat down. There was a sound in the church, expectant, presaging, like the stirring of leaves at the first breath of wind, and then all was silent.

II

He had preached for an hour - longer, perhaps. Alison could not have said how long. She had lost all sense of time.

No sooner had the text been spoken, "Except a man be born again, he cannot see the Kingdom of God," than she seemed to catch a fleeting glimpse of an hitherto unimagined Personality. Hundreds of times she had heard those words, and they had been as meaningless to her as to Nicodemus. But now - now something was brought home to her of the magnificent certainty with which they must first have been spoken, of the tone and bearing and authority of him who had uttered them. Was Christ like that? And could it be a Truth, after all, a truth only to be grasped by one who had experienced it?

It was in vain that man had tried to evade this, the supreme revelation of Jesus Christ, had sought to substitute ceremonies and sacrifices for spiritual rebirth. It was in vain that the Church herself had, from time to time, been inclined to compromise. St. Paul, once the strict Pharisee who had laboured for the religion of works, himself had been reborn into the religion of the Spirit. It was Paul who had liberated that message of rebirth, which the world has been so long in grasping, from the narrow bounds of Palestine and sent it ringing down the ages to the democracies of the twentieth century.

And even Paul, though not consciously inconsistent, could not rid himself completely of that ancient, automatic, conception of religion which the Master condemned, but had on occasions attempted fruitlessly to unite the new with the old. And thus, for a long time, Christianity had been wrongly conceived as history, beginning with what to Paul and the Jews was an historical event, the allegory of the Garden of Eden, the fall of Adam, and ending with the Jewish conception of the Atonement. This was a rationalistic and not a spiritual religion.

The miracle was not the vision, whatever its nature, which Saul beheld on the road to Damascus. The miracle was the result of that vision, the man reborn. Saul, the persecutor of Christians, become Paul, who spent the rest of his days, in spite of persecution and bodily infirmities, journeying tirelessly up and down the Roman Empire, preaching the risen Christ, and labouring more abundantly than they all! There was no miracle in the New Testament more wonderful than this.

The risen Christ! Let us not trouble ourselves about the psychological problems involved, problems which the first century interpreted in its own simple way. Modern, science has taught us this much, at least, that we have by no means fathomed the limits even of a transcendent personality. If proofs of the Resurrection and Ascension were demanded, let them be spiritual proofs, and there could be none more convincing than the life of the transformed Saul, who had given to the modern, western world the message of salvation . . . .

That afternoon, as Alison sat motionless on a distant hillside of the Park, gazing across the tree-dotted, rolling country to the westward, she recalled the breathless silence in the church when he had reached this point and paused, looking down at the congregation. By the subtle transmission of thought, of feeling which is characteristic at dramatic moments of bodies of people, she knew that he had already contrived to stir them to the quick. It was not so much that these opening words might have been startling to the strictly orthodox, but the added fact that Hodder had uttered them. The sensation in the pews, as Alison interpreted it and exulted over it, was one of bewildered amazement that this was their rector, the same man who had preached to them in June. Like Paul, of whom he spoke, he too was transformed, had come to his own, radiating a new power that seemed to shine in his face.

Still agitated, she considered that discourse now in her solitude, what it meant for him, for her, for the Church and civilization that a clergyman should have had the courage to preach it. He himself had seemed unconscious of any courage; had never once - she recalled - been sensational. He had spoken simply, even in the intensest moments of denunciation. And she wondered now how he had managed, without stripping himself, without baring the intimate, sacred experiences of his own soul, to convey to them, so nobly, the change which had taken place in him....

He began by referring to the hope with which he had come to St. John's, and the gradual realization that the church was a failure - a dismal failure when compared to the high ideal of her Master. By her fruits she should be known and judged. From the first he had contemplated, with a heavy heart, the sin and misery at their very gates. Not three blocks distant children were learning vice in the streets, little boys of seven and eight, underfed and anaemic, were driven out before dawn to sell newspapers, little girls thrust forth to haunt the saloons and beg, while their own children were warmed and fed. While their own daughters were guarded, young women in Dayton Street were forced to sell themselves into a life which meant slow torture, inevitable early death. Hopeless husbands and wives were cast up like driftwood by the cruel, resistless flood of modern civilization - the very civilization which yielded their wealth and luxury. The civilization which professed the Spirit of Christ, and yet was pitiless.

He confessed to them that for a long time he had been blind to the truth, had taken the inherited, unchristian view that the disease which caused vice and poverty might not be cured, though its ulcers might be alleviated. He had not, indeed, clearly perceived and recognized the disease. He had regarded Dalton Street in a very special sense as a reproach to St. John's, but now he saw that all such neighbourhoods were in reality a reproach to the city, to the state, to the nation. True Christianity and Democracy were identical, and the congregation of St. John's, as professed Christians and citizens, were doubly responsible, inasmuch as they not only made no protest or attempt to change a government which permitted the Dalton Streets to exist, but inasmuch also as, - directly or indirectly, - they derived a profit from conditions which were an abomination to God. It would be but an idle mockery for them to go and build a settlement house, if they did not first reform their lives.

Here there had been a decided stir among the pews. Hodder had not seemed to notice it.

When he, their rector, had gone to Dalton Street to

invite the poor and wretched into God's Church, he was met by the scornful question: "Are the Christians of the churches any better than we? Christians own the grim tenements in which we live, the saloons and brothels by which we are surrounded, which devour our children. Christians own the establishments which pay us starvation wages; profit by politics, and take toll from our very vice; evade the laws and reap millions, while we are sent to jail. Is their God a God who will lift us out of our misery and distress? Are their churches for the poor? Are not the very pews in which they sit as closed to us as their houses?"

"I know thy works, that thou art neither cold nor hot. I would thou wert cold or hot."

One inevitable conclusion of such a revelation was that he had not preached to them the vital element of Christianity. And the very fact that his presentation of religion had left many indifferent or dissatisfied was proof-positive that he had dwelt upon non-essentials, laid emphasis upon the mistaken interpretations of past ages. There were those within the Church who were content with this, who - like the Pharisees of old - welcomed a religion which did not interfere with their complacency, with their pursuit of pleasure and wealth, with their special privileges; welcomed a Church which didn't raise her voice against the manner of their lives - against the order, the Golden Calf which they had set up, which did not accuse them of deliberately retarding the coming of the Kingdom of God.

Ah, that religion was not religion, for religion was a spiritual, not a material affair. In that religion, vainly designed by man as a compromise between God and Mammon, there was none of the divine discontent of the true religion of the Spirit, no need of the rebirth of the soul. And those who held it might well demand, with Nicodemus and the rulers of the earth, "How can these things be?"

And there were others who still lingered in the Church, perplexed and wistful, who had come to him and confessed that the so-called catholic acceptance of divine truths, on which he had hitherto dwelt, meant nothing to them. To these, in particular, he owed a special reparation, and he took this occasion to announce a series of Sunday evening sermons on the Creeds. So long as the Creeds remained in the Prayer Book it was his duty to interpret them in terms not only of modern thought, but in harmony with the real significance of the Person and message of Jesus Christ. Those who had come to him questioning, he declared, were a thousand times right in refusing to accept the interpretations of other men, the consensus of opinion of more ignorant ages, expressed in an ancient science and an archaic philosophy.

And what should be said of the vast and ever increasing numbers of those not connected with the Church, who had left it or were leaving it? and of the less fortunate to whose bodily wants they had been ministering in the parish house, for whom it had no spiritual message, and who never entered its doors? The necessity of religion, of getting in touch with, of dependence on the Spirit of the Universe was inherent in man, and yet there were thousands - nay, millions in the nation to-day in whose hearts was an intense and unsatisfied yearning, who perceived no meaning in life, no Cause for which to work, who did not know what Christianity was, who had never known what it was, who wist not where to turn to find out. Education had brought many of them to discern, in the Church's teachings, an anachronistic medley of myths and legends, of theories of schoolmen and theologians, of surviving pagan superstitions which could not be translated into life. They saw, in Christianity, only the adulterations of the centuries. If any one needed a proof of the yearning people felt, let him go to the bookshops, or read in the publishers' lists to-day the announcements of books on religion. There was no supply where there was no demand.

Truth might no longer be identified with Tradition, and the day was past when councils and synods might determine it for all mankind. The era of forced acceptance of philosophical doctrines and dogmas was past, and that of freedom, of spiritual rebirth, of vicarious suffering, of willing sacrifice and service for a Cause was upon them. That cause was Democracy. Christ was uniquely the Son of God because he had lived and suffered and died in order to reveal to the world the meaning of this life and of the hereafter - the meaning not only for the individual, but for society as well. Nothing might be added to or subtracted from that message - it was complete.

True faith was simply trusting - trusting that Christ gave to the world the revelation of God's plan. And the Saviour himself had pointed out the proof: "If any man do his will, he shall know of the doctrine, whether it be of God, or whether I speak for myself." Christ had repeatedly rebuked those literal minds which had demanded material evidence: true faith spurned it, just as true friendship, true love between man and man, true trust scorned a written bond. To paraphrase St. James's words, faith without trust is dead - because faith without trust is impossible. God is a Spirit, only to be recognized in the Spirit, and every one of the Saviour's utterances were - not of the flesh, of the man - but of the Spirit within him. "He that hath seen me hath seen the Father; "and "Why callest thou me good? none is good save one, that is, God." The Spirit, the Universal Meaning of Life, incarnate in the human Jesus.

To be born again was to overcome our spiritual blindness, and then, and then only, we might behold the spirit shining in the soul of Christ. That proof had sufficed for Mark, had sufficed for the writer of the sublime Fourth Gospel, had sufficed for Paul. Let us lift this wondrous fact, once and for all, out of the ecclesiastical setting and incorporate it into our lives. Nor need the hearts of those who seek the Truth, who fear not to face it, be troubled if they be satisfied, from the Gospels, that the birth of Jesus was not miraculous. The physical never could prove the spiritual, which was the real and everlasting, which no discovery in science or history can take from us. The Godship of Christ rested upon no dogma, it was a conviction born into us with the new birth. And it becomes an integral part of our personality, our very being.

The secret, then, lay in a presentation of the divine message which would convince and transform and electrify those who heard it to action - a presentation of the message in terms which the age could grasp. That is what Paul had done, he had drawn his figures boldly from the customs of the life of his day, but a more or less intimate knowledge of these ancient customs were necessary before modern men and women could understand those figures and parallels. And the Church must awake to her opportunities, to her perception of the Cause. . . .

What, then, was the function, the mission of the Church Universal? Once she had laid claim to temporal power, believed herself to be the sole agency of God on earth, had spoken ex cathedra on philosophy, history, theology, and science, had undertaken to confer eternal bliss and to damn forever. Her members, and even her priests, had gone from murder to mass and from mass to murder, and she had engaged in cruel wars and persecutions to curtail the liberties of mankind. Under that conception religion was a form of insurance of the soul. Perhaps a common, universal belief had been necessary in the dark ages before the sublime idea of education for the masses had come; but the Church herself - through ignorance - had opposed the growth of education, had set her face sternly against the development of the individual, which Christ had taught, the privilege of man to use the faculties of the intellect which God had bestowed upon him. He himself, their rector, had advocated a catholic acceptance, though much modified from the mediaeval acceptance, - one that professed to go behind it to an earlier age. Yes, he must admit with shame that he had been afraid to trust where God trusted, had feared to confide the working out of the ultimate Truth of the minds of the millions.

The Church had been monarchical in form, and some strove stubbornly and blindly to keep her monarchical. Democracy in government was outstripping her. Let them look around, to-day, and see what was happening in the United States of America. A great movement was going on to transfer actual participation in government from the few to the many, - a movement towards true Democracy, and that was precisely what was about to happen in the Church. Her condition at present was one of uncertainty, transition - she feared to let go wholly of the old, she feared to embark upon the new. Just as the conservatives and politicians feared to give up the representative system, the convention, so was she afraid to abandon the synod, the council, and trust to man.

The light was coming slowly, the change, the rebirth of the Church by gradual evolution. By the grace of God those who had laid the foundations of the Church in which he stood, of all Protestantism, had built for the future. The racial instinct in them had asserted itself, had warned them that to suppress freedom in religion were to suppress it in life, to paralyze that individual initiative which was the secret of their advancement.

The new Church Universal, then, would be the militant, aggressive body of the reborn, whose mission it was to send out into the life of the nation transformed men and women who would labour unremittingly for the Kingdom of God. Unity would come - but unity in freedom, true Catholicity. The truth would gradually pervade the masses - be wrought out by them. Even the great evolutionary forces of the age, such as economic necessity, were acting to drive divided Christianity into consolidation, and the starving churches of country villages were now beginning to combine.

No man might venture to predict the details of the future organization of the united Church, although St. Paul himself had sketched it in broad outline: every worker, lay and clerical, labouring according to his gift, teachers, executives, ministers, visitors, missionaries, healers of sick and despondent souls. But the supreme function of the Church was to inspire - to inspire individuals to willing service for the cause, the Cause of Democracy, the fellowship of mankind. If she failed to inspire, the Church would wither and perish. And therefore she must revive again the race of inspirers, prophets, modern Apostles to whom this gift was given, going on their rounds, awaking cities and arousing whole country-sides.

But whence - it might be demanded by the cynical were the prophets to come? Prophets could not be produced by training and education; prophets must be born. Reborn, - that was the word. Let the Church have faith. Once her Cause were perceived, once her whole energy were directed towards its fulfilment, the prophets would arise, out of the East and out of the West, to stir mankind to higher effort, to denounce fearlessly the shortcomings and evils of the age. They had not failed in past ages, when the world had fallen into hopelessness, indifference, and darkness. And they would not fail now.

Prophets were personalities, and Phillips Brooks himself a prophet - had defined personality as a conscious relationship with God. "All truth," he had said, "comes to the world through personality." And down the ages had come an Apostolic Succession of personalities. Paul, Augustine, Francis, Dante, Luther, Milton, - yes, and Abraham Lincoln, and Phillips Brooks, whose Authority was that of the Spirit, whose light had so shone before men that they had glorified the Father which was in heaven; the current of whose Power had so radiated, in ever widening circles, as to make incandescent countless other souls.

And which among them would declare that Abraham Lincoln, like Stephen, had not seen his Master in the sky?

The true prophet, the true apostle, then, was one inspired and directed by the Spirit, the laying on of hands was but a symbol, - the symbol of the sublime truth that one personality caught fire from another. Let the Church hold fast to that symbol, as an acknowledgment, a reminder of a supreme mystery. Tradition had its value when it did not deteriorate into superstition, into the mechanical, automatic transmission characteristic of the mediaeval Church, for the very suggestion of which Peter had rebuked Simon in Samaria. For it would be remembered that Simon had said: "Give me also this power, that on whomsoever I lay hands, he may receive the Holy Ghost."

The true successor to the Apostles must be an Apostle himself.

Jesus had seldom spoken literally, and the truths he sought to impress upon the world had of necessity been clothed in figures and symbols, - for spiritual truths might be conveyed in no other way. The supreme proof of his Godship, of his complete knowledge of the meaning of life was to be found in his parables. To the literal, material mind, for example, the parable of the talents was merely an unintelligible case of injustice....What was meant by the talents? They were opportunities for service. Experience taught us that when we embraced one opportunity, one responsibility, the acceptance of it invariably led to another, and so the servant who had five talents, five opportunities, gained ten. The servant who had two gained two more. But the servant of whom only one little service was asked refused that, and was cast into outer darkness, to witness another performing the task which should have been his. Hell, here and hereafter, was the spectacle of wasted opportunity, and there is no suffering to compare to it.

The crime, the cardinal sin was with those who refused to serve, who shut their eyes to the ideal their Lord had held up, who strove to compromise with Jesus Christ himself, to twist and torture his message to suit their own notions as to how life should be led; to please God and Mammon at the same time, to bind Christ's Church for their comfort and selfish convenience. Of them it was written, that they shut up the Kingdom of Heaven against men; for they neither go in themselves, neither suffer them that are entering to go in. Were these any better than the people who had crucified the Lord for his idealism, and because he had not brought them the material Kingdom for which they longed?

That servant who had feared to act, who had hid his talent in the ground, who had said unto his lord, "I knew thee that thou art an hard man, reaping where thou hadst not sown," was the man without faith, the atheist who sees only cruelty and indifference in the order of things, who has no spiritual sight. But to the other servants it was said, "Thou halt been faithful over a few things, I will make thee ruler over many things. Enter thou into the joy of thy lord."

The meaning of life, then, was service, and by life our Lord did not mean mere human existence, which is only a part of life. The Kingdom of heaven is a state, and may begin here. And that which we saw around us was only one expression of that eternal life - a medium to work through, towards God. All was service, both here and hereafter, and he that had not discovered that the joy of service was the only happiness worth living for could have no conception of the Kingdom. To those who knew, there was no happiness like being able to say, "I have found my place in God's plan, I am of use." Such was salvation . . . .

And in the parable of the Prodigal Son may be read the history of what are known as the Protestant nations. What happens logically when the individual is suddenly freed from the restraint of external authority occurred when Martin Luther released the vital spark of Christianity, which he got from Paul, and from Christ himself - the revelation of individual responsibility, that God the Spirit would dwell, by grace, in the individual soul. Ah, we had paid a terrible yet necessary price for freedom. We had wandered far from the Father, we had been reduced to the very husks of individualism, become as swine. We beheld around us, to-day, selfishness, ruthless competition, as great contrasts between misery and luxury as in the days of the Roman Empire. But should we, for that reason, return to the leading-strings of authority? Could we if we would? A little thought ought to convince us that the liberation of the individual could not be revoked, that it had forever destroyed the power of authority to carry conviction. To go back to the Middle Ages would be to deteriorate and degenerate. No, we must go on. . . .

Luther's movement, in religion, had been the logical forerunner of democracy, of universal suffrage in government, the death-knell of that misinterpretation of Christianity as the bulwark of monarchy and hierarchy had been sounded when he said, "Ich kann nicht anders!" The new Republic founded on the western continent had announced to the world the initiation of the transfer of Authority to the individual soul. God, the counterpart of the King, the ruler in a high heaven of a flat terrestrial expanse, outside of the world, was now become the Spirit of a million spheres, the indwelling spirit in man. Democracy and the religion of Jesus Christ both consisted in trusting the man - yes, and the woman - whom God trusts. Christianity was individualism carried beyond philosophy into religion, and the Christian, the ideal citizen of the democracy, was free since he served not because he had to, but because he desired to of his own will, which, paradoxically, is God's will. God was in politics, to the confusion of politicians; God in government. And in some greater and higher sense than we had yet perceived, the saying 'vox populi vox dei' was eternally true. He entered into the hearts of people and moved them, and so the world progressed. It was the function of the Church to make Christians, until - when the Kingdom of God should come - the blending should be complete. Then Church and State would be identical, since all the members of the one would be the citizens of the other . . . .

"I will arise and go to my father." Rebirth! A sense of responsibility, of consecration. So we had come painfully through our materialistic individualism, through our selfish Protestantism, to a glimpse of the true Protestantism - Democracy.

Our spiritual vision was glowing clearer. We were beginning to perceive that charity did not consist in dispensing largesse after making a fortune at the expense of one's fellow-men; that there was something still wrong in a government that permits it. It was gradually becoming plain to us, after two thousand years, that human bodies and souls rotting in tenements were more valuable than all the forests on all the hills; that government, Christian government, had something to do with these.

We should embody, in government, those sublime words of the Master, "Suffer little children to come unto me." And the government of the future would care for the little children. We were beginning to do it. Here, as elsewhere, Christianity and reason went hand in hand, for the child became the man who either preyed on humanity and filled the prisons and robbed his fellows, or else grew into a useful, healthy citizen. It was nothing less than sheer folly as well as inhuman cruelty to let the children sleep in crowded, hot rooms, reeking with diseases, and run wild throughout the long summer, learning vice in the city streets. And we still had slavery - economic slavery - yes, and the more horrible slavery of women and young girls in vice - as much a concern of government as the problem which had confronted it in 1861 . . . . We were learning that there was something infinitely more sacred than property . . . .

And now Alison recalled, only to be thrilled again by an electric sensation she had never before experienced with such intensity, the look of inspiration on the preacher's face as he closed. The very mists of the future seemed to break before his importuning gaze, and his eyes seemed indeed to behold, against the whitening dawn of the spiritual age he predicted, the slender spires of a new Church sprung from the foundations of the old. A Church, truly catholic, tolerant, whose portals were wide in welcome to all mankind. The creative impulse, he had declared, was invariably religious, the highest art but the expression of the mute yearnings of a people, of a race. Thus had once arisen, all over Europe, those wonderful cathedrals which still cast their spell upon the world, and art to-day would respond - was responding - to the unutterable cravings of mankind, would strive once more to express in stone and glass and pigment what nations felt. Generation after generation would labour with unflagging zeal until the art sculptured fragment of the new Cathedral - the new Cathedral of Democracy - pointed upward toward the blue vault of heaven. Such was his vision - God the Spirit, through man reborn, carrying out his great Design . . .

CHAPTER XXII

"WHICH SAY TO THE SEERS, SEE NOT"

I

As Alison arose from her knees and made her way out of the pew, it was the expression on Charlotte Plimpton's face which brought her back once more to a sense of her surroundings; struck her, indeed, like a physical blow. The expression was a scandalized one. Mrs. Plimpton had moved towards her, as if to speak, but Alison hurried past, her exaltation suddenly shattered, replaced by a rising tide of resentment, of angry amazement against a materialism so solid as to remain unshaken by the words which had so uplifted her. Eddies were forming in the aisle as the people streamed slowly out of the church, and snatches of their conversation, in undertones, reached her ears.

"I should never have believed it!"

"Mr. Hodder, of all men. . ."

"The bishop!"

Outside the swinging doors, in the vestibule, the voices were raised a little, and she found her path blocked.

"It's incredible!" she heard Gordon Atterbury saying to little Everett Constable, who was listening gloomily.

"Sheer Unitarianism, socialism, heresy."

His attention was forcibly arrested by Alison, in whose cheeks bright spots of colour burned. He stepped aside, involuntarily, apologetically, as though he had instinctively read in her attitude an unaccountable disdain. Everett Constable bowed uncertainly, for Alison scarcely noticed them.

"Ahem!" said Gordon, nervously, abandoning his former companion and joining her, "I was just saying, it's incredible - "

She turned on him.

"It is incredible," she cried, "that persons who call themselves Christians cannot recognize their religion when they hear it preached."

He gave back before her, visibly, in an astonishment which would have been ludicrous but for her anger. He had never understood her - such had been for him her greatest fascination; - and now she was less comprehensible than ever. The time had been when he would cheerfully have given over his hope of salvation to have been able to stir her. He had never seen her stirred, and the sight of her even now in this condition was uncomfortably agitating. Of all things, an heretical sermon would appear to have accomplished this miracle!

"Christianity!" he stammered.

"Yes, Christianity." Her voice tingled. "I don't pretend to know much about it, but Mr. Hodder has at least made it plain that it is something more than dead dogmas, ceremonies, and superstitions."

He would have said something, but her one thought was to escape, to be alone. These friends of her childhood were at that moment so distasteful as to have become hateful. Some one laid a hand upon her arm.

"Can't we take you home, Alison? I don't see your motor."

It was Mrs. Constable.

"No, thanks - I'm going to walk," Alison answered, yet something in Mrs. Constable's face, in Mrs. Constable's voice, made her pause. Something new, something oddly sympathetic. Their eyes met, and Alison saw that the other woman's were tired, almost haggard - yet understanding.

"Mr. Hodder was right - a thousand times right, my dear," she said.

Alison could only stare at her, and the crimson in the bright spots of her cheeks spread over her face. Why had Mrs. Constable supposed that she would care to hear the sermon praised? But a second glance put her in possession of the extraordinary fact that Mrs. Constable herself was profoundly moved.

"I knew he would change," she went on, "I have seen for some time that he was too big a man not to change. But I had no conception that he would have such power, and such courage, as he has shown this morning. It is not only that he dared to tell us what we were - smaller men might have done that, and it is comparatively easy to denounce. But he has the vision to construct, he is a seer himself - he has really made me see what Christianity is. And as long as I live I shall never forget those closing sentences."

"And now?" asked Alison. "And now what will happen?"

Mrs. Constable changed colour. Her tact, on which she prided herself, had deserted her in a moment of unlooked-for emotion.

"Oh, I know that my father and the others will try to put him out - but can they?" Alison asked.

It was Mrs. Constable's turn to stare. The head she suddenly and impulsively put forth trembled on Alison's wrist.

"I don't know, Alison - I'm afraid they can. It is too terrible to think about. . . . And they can't - they won't believe that many changes are coming, that this is but one of many signs. . . Do come and see me."

Alison left her, marvelling at the passage between them, and that, of all persons in the congregation of St. John's, the lightning should have struck Mrs. Constable. . .

Turning to the right on Burton Street, she soon found herself walking rapidly westward through deserted streets lined by factories and warehouses, and silent in the Sabbath calm . . . . She thought of Hodder, she would have liked to go to him in that hour . . . .

In Park Street, luncheon was half over, and Nelson Langmaid was at the table with her father. The lawyer glanced at her curiously as she entered the room, and his usual word of banter, she thought, was rather lame. The two went on, for some time, discussing a railroad suit in Texas. And Alison, as she hurried through her meal, leaving the dishes almost untouched, scarcely heard them. Once, in her reverie, her thoughts reverted to another Sunday when Hodder had sat, an honoured guest, in the chair which Mr. Langmaid now occupied . . . .

It was not until they got up from the table that her father turned to her.

"Did you have a good sermon? " he asked.

It was the underlying note of challenge to which she responded.

"The only good sermon I have ever heard."

Their eyes met. Langmaid looked down at the tip of his cigar.

"Mr. Hodder," said Eldon Parr, "is to be congratulated."

II

Hodder, when the service was over, had sought the familiar recess in the robing-room, the words which he himself had spoken still ringing in his ears. And then he recalled the desperate prayer with which he had entered the pulpit, that it might be given him in that hour what to say: the vivid memories of the passions and miseries in Dalton Street, the sudden, hot response of indignation at the complacency confronting him. His voice had trembled with anger . . . . He remembered, as he had paused in his denunciation of these who had eyes and saw not, meeting the upturned look of Alison Parr, and his anger had turned to pity for their blindness - which once had been his own; and he had gone on and on, striving to interpret for them his new revelation of the message of the Saviour, to impress upon them the dreadful yet sublime meaning of life eternal. And it was in that moment the vision of the meaning of the evolution of his race, of the Prodigal turning to responsibility - of which he once had had a glimpse - had risen before his eyes in its completeness - the guiding hand of God in history! The Spirit in these complacent souls, as yet unstirred . . . .

So complete, now, was his forgetfulness of self, of his future, of the irrevocable consequences of the step he had taken, that it was only gradually he became aware that some one was standing near him, and with a start he recognized McCrae.

"There are some waiting to speak to ye," his assistant said.

"Oh!" Hodder exclaimed. He began, mechanically, to divest himself of his surplice. McCrae stood by.

"I'd like to say a word, first - if ye don't mind - " he began.

The rector looked at him quickly.

"I'd like just to thank ye for that sermon - I can say no more now," said McCrae; he turned away, and left the room abruptly.

This characteristic tribute from the inarticulate, loyal Scotchman left him tingling . . . . He made his way to the door and saw the people in the choir room, standing silently, in groups, looking toward him. Some one spoke to him, and he recognized Eleanor Goodrich.

"We couldn't help coming, Mr. Hodder - just to tell you how much we admire you. It was wonderful, what you said."

He grew hot with gratitude, with thankfulness that there were some who understood - and that this woman was among them, and her husband . . .Phil Goodrich took him by the hand.

"I can understand that kind of religion," he said. "And, if necessary, I can fight for it. I have come to enlist."

"And I can understand it, too," added the sunburned Evelyn. "I hope you will let me help."

That was all they said, but Hodder understood. Eleanor Goodrich's eyes were dimmed as she smiled an her sister and her husband - a smile that bespoke the purest quality of pride. And it was then, as they made way for others, that the full value of their allegiance was borne in upon him, and he grasped the fact that the intangible barrier which had separated him from them had at last been broken down: His look followed the square shoulders and aggressive, close-cropped head of Phil Goodrich, the firm, athletic figure of Evelyn, who had represented to him an entire class of modern young women, vigorous, athletic, with a scorn of cant in which he secretly sympathized, hitherto frankly untouched by spiritual interests of any sort. She had, indeed, once bluntly told him that church meant nothing to her . . . .

In that little company gathered in the choir room were certain members of his congregation whom, had he taken thought, he would least have expected to see. There were Mr. and Mrs. Bradley, an elderly couple who had attended St. John's for thirty years; and others of the same unpretentious element of his parish who were finding in modern life an increasingly difficult and bewildering problem. There was little Miss Tallant, an assiduous guild worker whom he had thought the most orthodox of persons; Miss Ramsay, who taught the children of the Italian mothers; Mr. Carton, the organist, a professed free-thinker, with whom Hodder had had many a futile argument; and Martha Preston, who told him that he had made her think about religion seriously for the first time in her life.

And there were others, types equally diverse. Young men of the choir, and others whom he had never seen, who informed him shyly that they would come again, and bring their friends . . . .

And all the while, in the background, Hodder had been aware of a familiar face - Horace Bentley's. Beside him, when at length he drew near, was his friend Asa Waring - a strangely contrasted type. The uncompromising eyes of a born leader of men flashed from beneath the heavy white eyebrows, the button of the Legion of Honour gleaming in his well-kept coat seemed emblematic of the fire which in his youth had driven him forth to fight for the honour of his country - a fire still undimmed. It was he who spoke first.

"This is a day I never expected to see, Mr. Hodder," he said, "for it has brought back to this church the man to whom it owes its existence. Mr. Bentley did more, by his labour and generosity, his true Christianity, his charity and his wisdom, for St. John's than any other individual. It is you who have brought him back, and I wish personally to express my gratitude."

Mr. Bentley, in mild reproof, laid his hand upon the t, shoulder of his old friend.

"Ah, Asa," he protested, "you shouldn't say such things."

"Had it not been for Mr. Bentley," Hodder explained, "I should not be here to-day."

Asa Waring pierced the rector with his eye, appreciating the genuine feeling with which these words were spoken. And yet his look contained a question.

"Mr. Bentley," Hodder added, "has been my teacher this summer."

The old gentleman's hand trembled a little on the goldheaded stick.

"It is a matter of more pride to me than I can express, sir, that you are the rector of this church with which my most cherished memories are associated," he said. "But I cannot take any part of the credit you give me for the splendid vision which you have raised up before us to-day, for your inspired interpretation of history, of the meaning of our own times. You have moved me, you have given me more hope and courage than I have had for many a long year - and I thank you, Mr. Hodder. I am sure that God will prosper and guide you in what you have so nobly undertaken."

Mr. Bentley turned away, walking towards the end of the room . . . .Asa Waring broke the silence.

"I didn't know that you knew him, that you had seen what he is doing - what he has done in this city. I cannot trust myself, Mr. Hodder, to speak of Horace Bentley's life. . . I feel too strongly on the subject. I have watched, year by year, this detestable spirit of greed, this lust for money and power creeping over our country, corrupting our people and institutions, and finally tainting the Church itself. You have raised your voice against it, and I respect and honour and thank you for it, the more because you have done it without resorting to sensation, and apparently with no thought of yourself. And, incidentally, you have explained the Christian religion to me as I have never had it explained in my life.

"I need not tell you you have made enemies - powerful ones. I can see that you are a man, and that you are prepared for them. They will leave no stone unturned, will neglect no means to put you out and disgrace you. They will be about your ears to-morrow - this afternoon, perhaps. I need not remind you that the outcome is doubtful. But I came here to assure you of my friendship and support in all you hope to accomplish in making the Church what it should be. In any event, what you have done to-day will be productive of everlasting good."

In a corner still lingered the group which Mr. Bentley had joined. And Hodder, as he made his way towards it, recognized the faces of some of those who composed it. Sally Grower was there, and the young women who lived in Mr. Bentley's house, and others whose acquaintance he had made during the summer. Mrs. Garvin had brought little Dicky, incredibly changed from the wan little figure he had first beheld in the stifling back room in Dalton Street; not yet robust, but freckled and tanned by the country sun and wind. The child, whom he had seen constantly in the interval, ran forward joyfully, and Hodder bent down to take his hand....

These were his friends, emblematic of the new relationship in which he stood to mankind. And he owed them to Horace Bentley! He wondered, as he greeted them, whether they knew what their allegiance meant to him in this hour. But it sufficed that they claimed him as their own.

Behind them all stood Kate Marcy. And it struck him for the first time, as he gazed at her earnestly, how her appearance had changed. She gave him a frightened, bewildered look, as though she were unable to identify him now with the man she had known in the Dalton Street flat, in the restaurant. She was still struggling, groping, wondering, striving to accustom herself to the higher light of another world.

"I wanted to come," she faltered. "Sally Grower brought me. . . "

Hodder went back with them to Dalton Street. His new ministry had begun. And on this, the first day of it, it was fitting that he should sit at the table of Horace Bentley, even as on that other Sunday, two years agone, he had gone to the home of the first layman of the diocese, Eldon Parr.

III

The peace of God passes understanding because sorrow and joy are mingled therein, sorrow and joy and striving. And thus the joy of emancipation may be accompanied by a heavy heart. The next morning, when Hodder entered his study, he sighed as his eye fell upon the unusual pile of letters on his desk, for their writers had once been his friends. The inevitable breach had come at last.

Most of the letters, as he had anticipated, were painful reading. And the silver paper-cutter with which he opened the first had been a Christmas present from Mrs. Burlingame, who had penned it, a lady of signal devotion to the church, who for many years had made it her task to supply and arrange the flowers on the altar. He had amazed and wounded her - she declared - inexpressibly, and she could no longer remain at St. John's - for the present, at least. A significant addition. He dropped the letter, and sat staring out of the window . . . presently arousing himself, setting himself resolutely to the task of reading the rest.

In the mood in which he found himself he did not atop to philosophize on the rigid yet sincere attitude of the orthodox. His affection for many of them curiously remained, though it was with some difficulty he strove to reconstruct a state of mind with which he had once agreed. If Christianity were to sweep on, these few unbending but faithful ones must be sacrificed: such was the law. . . Many, while repudiating his new beliefs - or unbeliefs! - added, to their regrets of the change in him, protestations of a continued friendship, a conviction of his sincerity. Others like Mrs. Atterbury, were frankly outraged and bitter. The contents of one lilac-bordered envelope brought to his eyes a faint smile. Did he know - asked the sender of this - could he know the consternation he had caused in so many persons, including herself? What was she to believe? And wouldn't he lunch with her on Thursday?

Mrs. Ferguson's letter brought another smile - more thoughtful. Her incoherent phrases had sprung from the heart, and the picture rose before him of the stout but frightened, good-natured lady who had never accustomed herself to the enjoyment of wealth and luxury. Mr. Ferguson was in such a state, and he must please not tell her husband that she had written. Yet much in his sermon had struck her as so true. It seemed wrong to her to have so much, and others so little! And he had made her remember many things in her early life she had forgotten. She hoped he would see Mr. Ferguson, and talk to him. . . .

Then there was Mrs. Constable's short note, that troubled and puzzled him. This, too, had in it an undercurrent of fear, and the memory came to him of the harrowing afternoon he had once spent with her, when she would have seemed to have predicted the very thing which had now happened to him. And yet not that thing. He divined instinctively that a maturer thought on the subject of his sermon had brought on an uneasiness as the full consequences of this new teaching had dawned upon her consequences which she had not foreseen when she had foretold the change. And he seemed to read between the lines that the renunciation he demanded was too great. Would he not let her come and talk to him? . . .

Miss Brewer, a lady of no inconsiderable property, was among those who told him plainly that if he remained they would have to give up their pews. Three or four communications were even more threatening. Mr. Alpheus Gore, Mrs. Plimpton's brother, who at five and forty had managed to triple his share of the Gore inheritance, wrote that it would be his regretful duty to send to the bishop an Information on the subject of Mr. Hodder's sermon.

There were, indeed, a few letters which he laid, thankfully, in a pile by themselves. These were mostly from certain humble members of his parish who had not followed their impulses to go to him after the service, or from strangers who had chanced to drop into the church. Some were autobiographical, such as those of a trained nurse, a stenographer, a hardware clerk who had sat up late Sunday night to summarize what that sermon had meant to him, how a gray and hopeless existence had taken on a new colour. Next Sunday he would bring a friend who lived in the same boarding house . . . . Hodder read every word of these, and all were in the same strain: at last they could perceive a meaning to religion, an application of it to such plodding lives as theirs . . . .

One or two had not understood, but had been stirred, and were coming to talk to him. Another was filled with a venomous class hatred. . . .

The first intimation he had of the writer of another letter seemed from the senses rather than the intellect. A warm glow suffused him, mounted to his temples as he stared at the words, turned over the sheet, and read at the bottom the not very legible signature. The handwriting, by no means classic, became then and there indelibly photographed on his brain, and summed up for him the characteristics, the warring elements in Alison Parr. "All afternoon," she wrote, "I have been thinking of your sermon. It was to me very wonderful - it lifted me out of myself. And oh, I want so much to believe unreservedly what you expressed so finely, that religion is democracy, or the motive power behind democracy - the service of humanity by the reborn. I understand it intellectually. I am willing to work for such a Cause, but there is something in me so hard that I wonder if it can dissolve. And then I am still unable to identify that Cause with the Church as at present constituted, with the dogmas and ceremonies that still exist. I am too thorough a radical to have your patience. And I am filled with rage - I can think of no milder word - on coming in contact with the living embodiments of that old creed, who hold its dogmas so precious. "Which say to the seers, See not; and to the prophets, Prophesy not unto us right things, speak unto us smooth things, prophesy deceits.'

"You see, I have been reading Isaiah, and when I came to that paragraph it seemed so appropriate. These people have always existed. And will they not always continue to exist? I wish I could believe, wholly and unreservedly, that this class, always preponderant in the world, could be changed, diminished - done away with in a brighter future! I can, at least, sympathize with Isaiah's wrath.

"What you said of the longing, the yearning which exists to-day amongst the inarticulate millions moved me most - and of the place of art in religion, to express that yearning. Religion the motive power of art, and art, too, service. 'Consider the lilies of the field.' You have made it, at least, all-comprehensive, have given me a new point of view for which I can never be sufficiently grateful - and at a time when I needed it desperately. That you have dared to do what you have done has been and will he an inspiration, not only to myself, but to many others. This, is a longer letter, I believe, than I have ever written in my life. But I wanted you to know."

He reread it twice, pondering over its phrases. "A new point of view....at a time when I needed it desperately." It was not until then that he realized the full intensity of his desire for some expression from her since the moment he had caught sight of her in the church. But he had not been prepared for the unreserve, the impulsiveness with which she had actually written. Such was his agitation that he did not heed, at first, a knock on the door, which was repeated. He thrust the letter inside his coat as the janitor of the parish house appeared.

"There is a gentleman to see you, sir, in the office," he said.

Hodder went down the stairs. And he anticipated, from the light yet nervous pacing that he heard on the bare floor, that the visitor was none other than his vestryman, Mr. Gordon Atterbury. The sight of the gentleman's spruce figure confirmed the guess.

"Good morning, Mr. Atterbury," he said as he entered.

Mr. Atterbury stopped in his steps, as if he had heard a shot.

"Ah - good morning, Mr. Hodder. I stopped in on my way to the office."

"Sit down," said the rector.

Mr. Atterbury sat down, but with the air of a man who does so under protest, who had not intended to. He was visibly filled and almost quivering with an excitement which seemed to demand active expression, and which the tall clergyman's physical calm and self-possession seemed to augment. For a moment Mr. Atterbury stared at the rector as he sat behind his desk. Then he cleared his throat.

"I thought of writing to you, Mr. Hodder. My mother, I believe, has done so. But it seemed to me, on second thought, better to come to you direct."

The rector nodded, without venturing to remark on the wisdom of the course.

"It occurred to me," Mr. Atterbury went on, "that possibly some things I wish to discuss might - ahem be dispelled in a conversation. That I might conceivably have misunderstood certain statements in your sermon of yesterday."

"I tried," said the rector, "to be as clear as possible."

"I thought you might not fully have realized the effect of what you said. I ought to tell you, I think, that as soon as I reached home I wrote out, as accurately as I could from memory, the gist of your remarks. And I must say frankly, although I try to put it mildly, that they appear to contradict and controvert the doctrines of the Church."

"Which doctrines?" Hodder asked.

Gordon Atterbury sputtered.

"Which doctrines?" he repeated. "Can it be possible that you misunderstand me? I might refer you to those which you yourself preached as late as last June, in a sermon which was one of the finest and most scholarly efforts I ever heard."

"It was on that day, Mr. Atterbury," replied the rector, with a touch of sadness in his voice, "I made the discovery that fine and scholarly efforts were not Christianity."

"What do you mean?" Mr. Atterbury demanded.

"I mean that they do not succeed in making Christians."

"And by that you imply that the members of your congregation, those who have been brought up and baptized and confirmed in this church, are not Christians?"

"I am sorry to say a great many of them are not," said the rector.

"In other words, you affirm that the sacrament of baptism is of no account."

"I affirm that baptism with water is not sufficient."

"I'm afraid that this is very grave," Mr. Hodder.

"I quite agree with you," replied the rector, looking straight at his vestryman.

"And I understood, - " the other went on, clearing his throat once more, "I think I have it correctly stated in my notes, but I wish to be quite clear, that you denied the doctrine of the virgin birth."

Hodder made a strong effort to control himself.

"What I have said I have said," he answered, "and I have said it in the hope that it might make some impression upon the lives of those to whom I spoke. You were one of them, Mr. Atterbury. And if I repeat and amplify my meaning now, it must be understood that I have no other object except that of putting you in the way of seeing that the religion of Christ is unique in that it is dependent upon no doctrine or dogma, upon no external or material sign or proof or authority whatever. I am utterly indifferent to any action you may contemplate taking concerning me. Read your four Gospels carefully. If we do not arrive, through contemplation of our Lord's sojourn on this earth, of his triumph over death, of his message - which illuminates the meaning of our lives here - at that inner spiritual conversion of which he continually speaks, and which alone will give us charity, we are not Christians."

"But the doctrines of the Church, which we were taught from childhood to believe? The doctrines which you once professed, and of which you have now made such an unlooked-for repudiation!"

"Yes, I have changed," said the rector, gazing seriously at the twitching figure of his vestryman, "I was bound, body and soul, by those very doctrines." He roused himself. "But on what grounds do you declare, Mr. Atterbury," he demanded, somewhat sternly, "that this church is fettered by an ancient and dogmatic conception of Christianity? Where are you to find what are called the doctrines of the Church? What may be heresy in one diocese is not so in another, and I can refer to you volumes written by ministers of this Church, in good standing, whose published opinions are the same as those I expressed in my sermon of yesterday. The very cornerstone of the Church is freedom, but many have yet to discover this, and we have held in our Communion men of such divergent views as Dr. Pusey and Phillips Brooks. Mr. Newman, in his Tract Ninety, which was sincerely written, showed that the Thirty-nine Articles were capable of almost any theological interpretation. From what authoritative source are we to draw our doctrines? In the baptismal service the articles of belief are stated to be in the Apostles' Creed, but nowhere - in this Church is it defined how their ancient language is to be interpreted. That is wisely left to the individual. Shall we interpret the Gospels by the Creeds, which in turn purport to be interpretations of the Gospels? Or shall we draw our conclusions as to what the Creeds may mean to us by pondering on the life of Christ, and striving to do his will? 'The letter killeth, but the Spirit maketh alive.'"

Hodder rose, and stood facing his visitor squarely. He spoke slowly, and the fact that he made no gesture gave all the more force to his words.

"Hereafter, Mr. Atterbury," he added, "so long as I am rector of this church, I am going to do my best to carry out the spirit of Christ's teaching - to make Christians. And there shall be no more compromise, so far as I can help it."

Gordon Atterbury had grown very pale. He, too, got to his feet.

"I - I cannot trust myself to discuss this matter with you any further, Mr. Hodder. I feel too deeply - too strongly on the subject. I do not pretend to account for this astonishing transformation in your opinions. Up to the present I have deemed St. John's fortunate - peculiarly fortunate, in having you for its rector. I am bound to say I think you have not considered, in this change of attitude on your part, those who have made St. John's what it is, who through long and familiar association are bound to it by a thousand ties, - those who, like myself, have what may be called a family interest in this church. My father and mother were married here, I was baptized here. I think I may go so far as to add, Mr. Hodder, that this is our church, the church which a certain group of people have built in which to worship God, as was their right. Nor do I believe we can be reproached with a lack of hospitality or charity. We maintain this parish house, with its clubs; and at no small inconvenience to ourselves we have permitted the church to remain in this district. There is no better church music in this city, and we have a beautiful service in the evening at which, all pews are free. It is not unreasonable that we should have something to say concerning the doctrine to be preached here, that we should insist that that doctrine be in accordance with what we have always believed was the true doctrine as received by this Church."

Up to this point Mr. Atterbury had had a feeling that he had not carried out with much distinction the programme which he had so carefully rehearsed on the way to the parish house. Hodder's poise had amazed and baffled him - he had expected to find the rector on the defensive. But now, burning anew with a sense of injustice, he had a sense at last of putting his case strongly.

The feeling of triumph, however, was short lived. Hodder did not reply at once. So many seconds, indeed, went by that Mr. Atterbury began once more to grow slightly nervous under the strange gaze to which he was subjected. And when the clergyman' spoke there was no anger in his voice, but a quality - a feeling which was disturbing, and difficult to define.

"You are dealing now, Mr. Atterbury," he said, "with the things of Caesar, not of God. This church belongs to God - not to you. But you have consecrated it to him. His truth, as Christ taught it, must not be preached to suit any man's convenience. When you were young you were not taught the truth - neither was I. It was mixed with adulterations which obscured and almost neutralized it. But I intend to face it now, and to preach it, and not the comfortable compromise which gives us the illusion that we are Christians because we subscribe to certain tenets, and permits us to neglect our Christian duties.

"And since you have spoken of charity, let me assure you that there is no such thing as charity without the transforming, personal touch. It isn't the bread or instruction or amusement we give people vicariously, but the effect of our gift - even if that gift be only a cup of cold water - in illuminating and changing their lives. And it will avail any church little to have a dozen settlement houses while her members acquiesce in a State which refuses to relieve her citizens from sickness and poverty. Charity bends down only to lift others up. And with all our works, our expenditure and toil, how many have we lifted up?"

Gordon Atterbury's indignation got the better of him. For he was the last man to behold with patience the shattering of his idols.

"I think you have cast an unwarranted reflection on those who have built and made this church what it is, Mr. Hodder," he exclaimed. "And that you will find there are in it many - a great many earnest Christians who were greatly shocked by the words you spoke yesterday, who will not tolerate any interference with their faith. I feel it my duty to speak frankly, Mr Hodder, disagreeable though it be, in view of our former relations. I must tell you that I am not alone in the opinion that you should resign. It is the least you can do, in justice to us, in justice to yourself. There are other bodies - I cannot call them churches - which doubtless would welcome your liberal, and I must add atrophying, interpretation of Christianity. And I trust that reflection will convince you of the folly of pushing this matter to the extreme. We should greatly deplore the sensational spectacle of St. John's being involved in an ecclesiastical trial, the unpleasant notoriety into which it would bring a church hitherto untouched by that sort of thing. And I ought to tell you that I, among others, am about to send an Information to the bishop."

Gordon Atterbury hesitated a moment, but getting no reply save an inclination of the head, took up his hat.

"Ahem - I think that is all I have to say, Mr. Hodder. Good morning."

Even then Hodder did not answer, but rose and held open the door. As he made his exit under the strange scrutiny of the clergyman's gaze the little vestryman was plainly uncomfortable. He cleared his throat once more, halted, and then precipitately departed.

Hodder went to the window and thoughtfully watched the hurrying figure of Mr. Atterbury until it disappeared, almost skipping, around the corner . . . . The germ of truth, throughout the centuries, had lost nothing of its dynamic potentialities. If released and proclaimed it was still powerful enough to drive the world to insensate anger and opposition....

As he stood there, lost in reflection, a shining automobile drew up at the curb, and from it descended a firm lady in a tight-fitting suit whom he recognized as Mrs Wallis Plimpton. A moment later she had invaded the office - for no less a word may be employed to express her physical aggressiveness, the glowing health which she radiated.

"Good morning, Mr. Hodder," she said, seating herself in one of the straight-backed chairs. "I have been so troubled since you preached that sermon yesterday, I could scarcely sleep. And I made up my mind I'd come to you the first thing this morning. Mr. Plimpton and I have been discussing it. In fact, people are talking of nothing else. We dined with the Laureston Greys last night, and they, too, were full of it." Charlotte Plimpton looked at him, and the flow of her words suddenly diminished. And she added, a little lamely for her, "Spiritual matters in these days are so difficult, aren't they?"

"Spiritual matters always were difficult, Mrs. Plimpton," he said.

"I suppose so," she assented hurriedly, with what was intended for a smile. "But what I came to ask you is this - what are we to teach our children?"

"Teach them the truth," the rector replied.

"One of the things which troubled me most was your reference to modern criticism," she went on, recovering her facility. "I was brought up to believe that the Bible was true. The governess - Miss Standish, you know, such a fine type of Englishwoman - reads the children Bible stories every Sunday evening. They adore them, and little Wallis can repeat them almost by heart - the pillar of cloud by day, Daniel in the lions' den, and the Wise Men from the East. If they aren't true, some one ought to have told us before now."

A note of injury had crept into her voice.

"How do you feel about these things yourself?" Holder inquired.

"How do I feel? Why, I have never thought about them very much - they were there, in the Bible!"

"You were taught to believe them?"

"Of course," she exclaimed, resenting what seemed a reflection on the Gore orthodoxy.

"Do they in any manner affect your conduct?"

"My conduct?" she repeated. "I don't know what you mean. I was brought up in the church, and Mr. Plimpton has always gone, and we are bringing up the children to go. Is that what you mean?"

"No," Hodder answered, patiently, "that is not what I mean. I ask whether these stories in any way enter into your life, become part of you, and tend to make you a more useful woman?"

"Well - I have never considered them in that way," she replied, a little perplexed.

"Do you believe in them yourself?"

"Why - I don't know, - I've never thought. I don't suppose I do, absolutely - not in those I have mentioned."

"And you think it right to teach things to your children which you do not yourself believe?"

"How am I to decide?" she demanded.

"First by finding out yourself what you do believe," he replied, with a touch of severity.

"Mr. Hodder!" she cried in a scandalized voice, "do you mean to say that I, who have been brought up in this church, do not know what Christianity is."

He looked at her and shook his head.

"You must begin by being honest with yourself," he went on, not heeding her shocked expression. "If you are really in earnest in this matter, I should be glad to help you all I can. But I warn you there is no achievement in the world more difficult than that of becoming a, Christian. It means a conversion of your whole being something which you cannot now even imagine. It means a consuming desire which, - I fear, -

in consideration of your present mode of life, will be difficult to acquire."

"My present mode of life!" she gasped.

"Precisely," said the rector. He was silent, regarding, her. There was discernible not the slightest crack of crevice in the enamel of this woman's worldly armour.

For the moment her outraged feelings were forgotten. The man had fascinated her. To be told, in this authoritative manner, that she was wicked was a new and delightful experience. It brought back to her the real motive of her visit, which had in reality been inspired not only by the sermon of the day before, but by sheer curiosity.

"What would you have me do?" she demanded.

"Find yourself."

"Do you mean to say that I am not - myself?" she asked, now completely bewildered.

"I mean to say that you are nobody until you achieve conviction."

For Charlotte Plimpton, nee Gore, to be told in her own city, by the rector of her own church that she was nobody was an event hitherto inconceivable! It was perhaps as extraordinary that she did not resent. it. Curiosity still led her on.

"Conviction?" she repeated. "But I have conviction, Mr. Hodder. I believe in the doctrines of the Church."

"Belief!" he exclaimed, and checked himself strongly. "Conviction through feeling. Not until then will you find what you were put in the world for."

"But my husband - my children? I try to do my duty."

"You must get a larger conception of it," Hodder replied.

"I suppose you mean," she declared, "that I am to spend the rest of my life in charity."

"How you would spend the rest of your life would be revealed to you," said the rector.

It was the weariness in his tone that piqued her now, the intimation that he did not believe in her sincerity - had not believed in it from the first. The life-long vanity of a woman used to be treated with consideration, to be taken seriously, was aroused. This extraordinary man had refused to enter into the details which she inquisitively craved.

Charlotte Plimpton rose.

"I shall not bother you any longer at present, Mr. Hodder," she said sweetly. "I know you must have, this morning especially, a great deal to trouble you."

He met her scrutiny calmly.

"It is only the things we permit to trouble us that do so, Mrs. Plimpton," he replied. "My own troubles have arisen largely from a lack of faith on the part of those whom I feel it is my duty to influence."

It was then she delivered her parting shot, which she repeated, with much satisfaction, to her husband that evening. She had reached the door. Was there a special service at Calvary yesterday?" she asked innocently, turning back.

"Not that I know of."

"I wondered. Mr. Parr was there; I'm told - and he's never been known to desert St. John's except on the rarest occasions. But oh, Mr. Hodder, I must congratulate you on your influence with Alison. When she has been out here before she never used to come to church at all."

www.ingramcontent.com/pod-product-compliance
Lightning Source LLC
Chambersburg PA
CBHW020547310726
48979CB00008B/1119/J

* 9 7 8 1 4 2 1 8 0 6 9 4 5 *